Stories by Contemporary Writers from Shanghai

Breathing

T0095996

This book is edited and designed by the Editorial Committee of *Cultural China* series

Text by Sun Ganlu
Translation by Zhu Jisong

Cover Image by Quanjing
Interior Design by Xue Wenqing
Cover Design by Wang Wei

Editor: Wu Yuezhou
Editorial Director: Zhang Yicong

Senior Consultants: Sun Yong, Wu Ying, Yang Xinci
Managing Director and Publisher: Wang Youbu

ISBN: 978-1-60220-256-6

Address any comments about *Breathing* to:

Better Link Press
99 Park Ave
New York, NY 10016
USA

or

Shanghai Press and Publishing Development Company
F 7 Donghu Road, Shanghai, China (200031)
Email: comments_betterlinkpress@hotmail.com

Printed in China by Shenzhen Donneiley Printing Co., Ltd.

1   3   5   7   9   10   8   6   4   2

Breathing

By Sun Ganlu
Translated by Zhu Jisong

Better Link Press

Foreword

This collection of books for English readers consists of short stories and novellas published by writers based in Shanghai. Apart from a few who are immigrants to Shanghai, most of them were born in the city, from the latter part of the 1940s to the 1980s. Some of them had their works published in the late 1970s and the early 1980s; some gained recognition only in the 21st century. The older among them were the focus of the "To the Mountains and Villages" campaign in their youth, and as a result, lived and worked in the villages. The difficult paths of their lives had given them unique experiences and perspectives prior to their eventual return to Shanghai. They took up creative writing for different reasons but all share a creative urge and a love for writing. By profession, some of them are college professors, some literary editors, some directors of literary institutions, some freelance writers and some professional writers. From the individual styles of the authors and the art of their writings, readers can easily detect traces of the authors' own experiences in life, their interests, as well as their aesthetic values. Most of the works in this collection are still written in the realistic style that represents, in a painstakingly fashioned fictional world, the changes of the times in urban and rural life. Having grown up in a more open era, the younger writers have been spared the hardships experienced by their predecessors, and therefore seek greater freedom in their writing. Whatever category of writers they belong to, all of them have gained their rightful places in Chinese literary circles over the last forty years. Shanghai writers tend to favor urban narratives more than other genres of writing. Most of the works in this collection can be characterized as urban literature with Shanghai characteristics, but there are also exceptions.

Called the "Paris of the East," Shanghai was already an international metropolis in the 1920s and 30s. Being the center of China's economy, culture and literature at the time, it housed a majority of writers of importance in the history of modern Chinese literature. The list includes Lu Xun, Guo Moruo, Mao Dun and Ba Jin, who had all written and published prolifically in Shanghai. Now, with Shanghai re-emerging as a globalized metropolis, the Shanghai writers who have appeared on the literary scene in the last forty years all face new challenges and literary quests of the times. I am confident that some of the older writers will produce new masterpieces. As for the fledging new generation of writers, we naturally expect them to go far in their long writing careers ahead of them. In due course, we will also introduce those writers who did not make it into this collection.

Wang Jiren
Series Editor

Volume I

1

"Goodbye, Luo Ke," said his lover's husband courteously after announcing the bad news, quitting the dull conversation on the other end of the phone. Luo Ke, a somnambulist, found himself possessed by the God of Crying. He left her behind in a summer, just as he was coming back now to the beginning of his love journey in grief. The lingering midday melancholy stemmed from his prayers for passion. Now his yearning, after the last encounter in the last year of the decade, was nothing but an ornament on the desk. The imploration on that Europeanized morning withering into the remote, he had nothing to forsake, apart from ice and a poem of the sleeping heart, on the bank of this filthy southern river. The distant nation had no longer anything mysterious, except the music in the room and the raindrops of September outside the windows. For Luo Ke, the journey to the foreign land was like a page falling out of a book, and that night was just one for requiem. He imagined himself talking on a mountain and meditating upon the surface of a river. For him, this story would become the appendix to the archives of his monologues. All the days were overlaid with each other in the way that their skins, as well as the nerves underneath, were combined. Their encounter was like a wall chart of human organs, portraying rivers of blood vessels, the capital of the heart and the invisible breath of love. Once in an autumn, he wondered whether this was a city of sufferings and whether he would compare the coming winter to a bunch of rosemary. Luo Ke hung up the phone with a sigh. Everything was gone.

Luo Ke pulled his index finger out of the hardcover *Selected Poems of Charles Baudelaire*, recalling everything it had touched. Smoke was curling up from the half-smoked cigarette on the white rim of the ceramic ashtray. Not thoroughly burned, it was still sending out the choking smoke. He took some bare-footed steps, following the pattern on the floor, and pushed open the windows that had been left ajar. The luxuriant foliage of the oriental planes came into his view, and along came his recollections of the past. Quiet in the street, the siren of an ocean liner penetrated into the room from faraway, which sounded like a sob. Clearing his dry throat, he thought the man by the windows, who had just woken up from a dream, might be a combination of a chicken and a Western court jester. Yin Mang, his guide, told him from the beginning that he had a prideful strong jaw. The moment he pushed open the windows in the night breeze, feelings of dejection swelled in him, awakening him from a whole afternoon's reading. Baudelaire's theme was bohemian, and anything other than that he had forgotten. The summary concluded by overlooking the obscure narration was simply interrupted by a phone call. Luo Ke considered that it was Yin Mang, not her husband, that hung up the phone in Sidney, just as she once cut the call to her mother with her silky arm reaching out over his body.

Luo Ke recalled all the international calls he received on various occasions and in different seasons of the past year. Fälön, Macao, Sidney, New York—these names were all followed by some other combinations of Chinese characters, names of people. Those pleasant conversations would turn awkward in an instant because of the distance. "I hate this room." Luo Ke intended to employ some more abstract spatial concepts, but he meant to provoke Xiang An, who was wrapped in a bed sheet. "I can stop smoking, but you didn't need to get so mad with me." She was to continue, but the following smoking interrupted everything.

They stayed all day in this room packed with books and all kinds of luxury items. It must be these shiny black electrical appliances that provoked her, or the Mortrie piano covered by a piece of maroon flannel, with its yellowed keys vaguely betraying its age and dignity. Otherwise, it might be the portable English typewriter, which remained open. Most probably, it was the dust on the furniture. "Your mysophobia and inferiority complex!" Luo Ke already shouted at her at dinner last night. Cluttered with a Yugoslavian ashtray, a stack of photos with no human figures, a crystal glass pig whose shape was exaggerated, a bunch of reeds, dozens of paperback novels all in a pile, the room seemed to be mocking at her intelligence. Experience taught her that tidiness was the external sign of a well-off life and the cult of order, or at least, it was the metonym for banknotes. The rubber plant in the glazed black pot that measured about 2 feet in diameter was growing crazily in the summer sunshine. Its big, thick, dark green leaves were as sexy as the tongues of Turks, the top of which had reached the whitewashed ceiling. Xiang An immersed herself in staring at nothingness. The smell of sweat was still lingering on her dark red skin. She could smell his scent, which brought back her fresh memory of everything, the shape of his right middle finger, the outline of the left ear, the pink halo around the earlobes, the layers of his hair, his robust collarbones, tightened back muscles, the sweat oozing from his chest and the mesmerizing light shining to his eyes. All of these were revealed in her moaning. At this moment, she sighed, as if her lungs were filled with the praise of the tobacco.

Luo Ke, naked, bent over the faux rosewood desk with his shirt lying on it. He tilted his head and started writing a letter. He knew that if he spent time searching out his socks, this letter to Sidney might never come into being. The curtains in Yin Mang's house were azure blue with milky white spots, which formed distorted constellations and random patterns. The past years rendered them fragile. They were ripped apart like paper by wind and time and ended up as mop strings in the bathroom. The shining spark in the horizon faraway produced a dark brown gloss on the floor. The room became completely dim. Her voice, gentle yet a little hoarse, resurfaced in the falling darkness. The odorous mixture of the flue-cured tobacco and oriental plane leaves was dry and bitter, lingering on the tip of his tongue, which formed a tiny swirl of senses. What shall be written on this clean paper? Gradually, the scene in Luo Ke's imagination replaced his unwritten narration—a chair facing the sun, a spotless road, a spiral staircase, an abandoned cloister, the antechamber of a shrine, people standing still on a plaza, pine trees in a yard, woods in the sunset, apartment windows, gentle arches, women and their shades, the collar and buttons of a shirt, heels of leather shoes ... In a word, it was a colonial scene. The scenery in these pictures was related to the European civilization; it was a kind of conceptual sculpture distant from him. Like the more remote scenery behind Yin Mang, who was far away, Luo Ke could not include a set of symbols into a short letter to his deceased lover. The curtains fluttered in the darkness, seemingly stirred by the vibrating pressure of the car wheels on the road outside. "There must be a large crowd of women fascinated by your immersion in meditation, such as me." Xiang An pulled off the bed sheet, exposing her entire body. She put on her blouse, turned on the radio, and walked around in the room, wandering and fumbling. Indulging in the rustling sound, Luo Ke fell into an absolute peace.

2

His house, or to be exact his father's house, or the shelter of their family, was an old foreign-style villa in disrepair. This three-storied house with a lawn, a relic of the former French Concession, finally became a hat stand for hanging vague signs of pedigrees after being exposed to elements for over half a century. The villa, with sealed fireplaces and dim corridors stuffed with clutter, was inhabited by three families. The room upstairs lived a proud tenor and a group of fans of high C, who were also his admirers under his leadership. "My husband is able to remain on high A for ten bars, and the same with High C." Downstairs lived a dentist who had hung out his shingle. The bald dentist was a widower, relentlessly skilled with his appliances. In short, each family's dominator practiced in a profession related to the human oral cavity. The small building was at the end of a deep and winding alley, like some organ of a human body. It was a daily routine to hear Concone's etudes or the folk music, the moaning and screaming from time to time at the dentist's, mixed with play lines in constant modification.

This unbearable fortress, made up of the cruel medical science and the voice blender who used his high pitch to dominate his family, was particularly quiet at the moment. "Do your parents often go travelling?" asked Xiang An, her voice accompanied by the violin music on the radio, as if it were a repeatedly rehearsed lyric. "This is the first time," answered Luo Ke lazily, avoiding the boring story of his pedigree. She moved to his back, gently inserting her fingers into his thick hair. Little by little, encouraged by the darkness, she held his head by her breast. The fragrance of the soap after the shower last night now turned into the smell of hay. "Are you always like this, missing another woman, or even more than one woman, while staying with one?" She gazed at Luo Ke's eyes from above. He genuinely appreciated it, as from this angle, he almost completely discovered the dreamy quality of women. The dreaminess produced by the reversal of the position happened to reveal the essence of the true image after restoration. She came face to face with him, while her body knocked off the *Selected Poems of Charles Baudelaire* on the edge of the desk. The narration of a debauched life was initiated on the floor. A certain page fluttered and dropped in the breeze from the window. The scent of ink and paper wafted around their naked ankles. The sound of paper scraping the floor awakened the vague desire deep down. On the radio was the affected voice of a female broadcaster, and after seconds of silence, suddenly a horn announced the beginning of another piece of music.

A black-and-white photo of Luo Ke's father was hung above the bookcase. In the wooden frame, he was smoking in a cold manner, eyes staring vacantly. He had written thirty plays and nearly a hundred sonorous lyric poems about agricultural machinery and heavy industry in his life. His industriousness rivaled that of Shakespeare, in a sharp contrast with his only son, Luo Ke's idling about. Ten years ago, Luo Yizhi, a playwright, or a dramatist, started living a secluded life at home, buried in writing his memoir. Those histories of bitterness and struggles were nothing more than the dim recollections of Luo Ke's landlord grandfather, poetic touches to the age-old romantic affairs, plus illegible diaries, carefully collected postcards, yellowed newspaper clippings, some unfamiliar neologisms, and long paragraphs of explanation excerpted from encyclopedias—in short, trivialities that his undutiful son would not care to collect. "It is indeed surprising that this man from Sichuan (a province south-west of China), eccentric in taste and addicted to spicy food should become a colleague of Bertolt Brecht." Luo Ke had made this remark to almost every girlfriend of his in different periods. As to himself, the thin man drown in endless sensual pleasure was no doubt the fruit of his parents' love, their daily vexation, the bane of their elderly lives and the subject of reproach when they felt down. "You'll never know what dedication means," said Xiang An while biting his lips. Luo Ke suddenly felt exhausted, the craving for sleep running in his blood vessels all the way to his brain. "It is as if the story between you and me were happening between another couple, and became a part of another story." "I want some water." Xiang An interrupted him, left his side and walked towards the seven milky white teacups on the floor beside the bed. When she crouched down, Luo Ke felt how badly he missed the heat and flesh of her body, and the hesitation of her caressing fingers from shyness to boldness. When she gracefully turned her palm and rubbed his body with the small joints on back of her hand, Luo Ke felt as if he suddenly lifted his head from immersion in the seawater and hurriedly took a small breath of the air above the surface. But instantly the sea vanished. Luo Ke seemed to be watching over the rough sea from a solitary altitude. The evening breeze sent a chill to his bare chest, meanwhile leaving a sense of scorching on his heart as well as his skin. Undoubtedly, she was the most cherished woman in his life. Luo Ke wanted to tell her this immediately, but almost at the same time, he gave up the idea.

3

Their first date took place in the library where Xiang An worked. Gombrich's work made Luo Ke tired, who stopped reading at the chapter "Looking Eastwards," and decided to save the content of Islam, China, and the history from the second to the thirteenth century to the next time. The afternoon sun had moved away from the window, and the couple across from him browsing through pictorials had been away for a while. Through the huge window on his right side he could see the lawn of the park outside the library. The park was not crowded with people; thus the rustling of camphor trees was distinct. Further afield was a downtown plaza, where a boy about ten years old was roller-skating on one side of the road. Everything seemed motionless to Luo Ke, who had lived in this coastal city for decades. He realized it was this thought, not Gombrich's bulky hardcover, that had made him tired. Luo Ke looked across the numerous old chairs in the reading hall at where Xiang An sat. She was helping a middle-aged reader to search for a book and her seat was vacant. There would still be a while before the library closed. A sad feeling pervaded the quiet hall. For Luo Ke, the daily waiting had a strong implication, which contained both the irony of the longing for eternity and the exhortation on momentary experiences. The library was a symbol to him, a miniature of people writing painstakingly or freely in countless times, and also a portrayal of the long-time dreariness that accompanied writing.

It allowed the various records and personal narrations of all ages to cluster together in silence and become a normal scene of the library. It was a labyrinth for intelligence, a blessed place full of danger and exceeding beauty, a paradise of loss filled with signs but no tracks, a winding outlet for emotions, a language checkerboard with complex rules, a daunting boardinghouse for souls, a factory of knowledge trinkets, an indoor park or a cloister divided by bookshelves, and a graveyard of life made up of paper, ink and writing.

Watching the slender figure of the woman he was so infatuated with reappear from behind a row of bookshelves, Luo Ke suddenly yearned to get in a relationship. She smiled at him, and turned around to the middle-aged man in a brown leather jacket. In Luo Ke's eyes, she was covering her absent-mindedness with a look of concentration. The equally distributed lighting in the reading hall highlighted the pallor of her fair skin, and her eyelids with dark shades indicated weariness. When this woman, a fan of apple, cotton underwear, and TV, and an affectionate lover, remained silent, the soft lines on her face would offer an illusion that the word "crazy" was so obnoxious that it had never existed in her dictionary. Now and then there were sounds of footsteps and of the colliding chairs of the readers who hurried to leave at the last minute before the library closed. It was in this kind of environment with a little musty smell that she started a relationship with the man she fell in love with.

4

This place, connected with a dignified and elusive history, always evoked Luo Ke's condensed memories of his own short history. Its book collections and serenity often reminded Luo Ke of reading Guo Moruo's sputtering poems towards the noisy kids on the makeshift podium on the playground when he was in elementary school. At the age of nine, Luo Ke started longing for friendships with adults of the opposite gender and at the age of twelve, he refused to go to public baths. Another thing connected with his boyhood memories was his preference for plastic sandals. Luo Ke served four years in the anti-aircraft artillery unit on an island with the duty of reloading, during which they once went to Indochina. With subtropical jungles, humid air, steaming palms leaves under the scorching sun, U.S. B-52 bombers roaring past above his head, the horror in his memory, and bodies of young soldiers, Vietnam was a country he could barely describe. Among his collections there was a toy plane made of the remains of a Phantom Jet brought down. It was carefully kept in an old biscuit tin, accompanied by over one hundred exquisite Mao Zedong badges. Before the age of twenty, Luo Ke was accessible to *Gao Yubao* and the tragedies and paeans by the playwright Luo Yizhi. Apart from this intellectual staple food, he also searched for desserts for his soul. This list of heavy desserts usually included the complete twenty illustrated volumes of *The Golden Lotus* (a secret collection of his father), *Slapping the Table in Amazement,* which he had learnt by heart, and another book that was worth mentioning—the rural version of *Handbook for Barefoot Doctors.* These remarkable works were now lying on a shelf in the row facing south. They seemed so elegant and dignified when not being read by people. They became sleepers, as those famous authors. For many times, Luo Ke, as a teenager, had sneaked into his father's study when he was out, as if getting over a stone-stacked barrier, over the fingers in the pages, over the straw hat, leaves and other things and reaching the inscription of the sexual desire. He once touched these pictographs and felt the damage inflicted on the poems and skin, like witnessing a fulfilling journey of love, like a hive and an expected voyage. Luo Ke's vision was a string on the violin, a tree in the middle of a street, and the same as several stationary scenes. He felt like a street lamp in the old times, a courtyard, the border areas from a bird's eye view, a straight line symbolizing the surface of water; on his margin was a vine and a thought, entangling stones and the covers of those sleeping books. The reading nights were now intertwined into an abstract pattern, like kangaroos and leaps on the grass, like rings and the fate. The home of the dead was in the grass of the graveyard. Now death was a faraway song, the faces in the ceremony, the yearning and those heart-shaped ornaments. He and his young companion, Yin Mang, were once excited about writing. But at this moment, Luo Ke felt like an ancient poet, and under his pen there were only some blank papers. The talk under the tree, a ripple in the cup and a silent walk under the clouds and shades eventually became an album under a waterfall and the melancholy on a hard stone. He was once immersed in books and dreams, watching the school gate and the room window and waiting for Yin Mang to sit in his embrace. He asked her what kind of payment the people working for themselves were waiting for. An unlit waxwork or the coldest but also the warmest night of all? A remarkable surname, a place, the number that recorded the year, or the indiscernible ray of sunlight that shone into their heart? No, it was silence, he thought. It was a statue that no longer uttered a sound, as death was the most enduring praise and the greatest meditation, and as if facing the desolation and darkness in front of the door in suspense. Luo Ke said to Yin Mang in his heart, "I was a gift of yours, like a chime for compensation, a wooden photo frame, a wish, a wind-bell and a photo that would possibly be taken together." They once started between two endings, and now they ended after the final beginning.

5

At this moment, the lights on the nearby commercial street were barely lit. In the eyes of Xiang An's aunt, who was from Hong Kong and would just spend the rest of her life watching TV, it was a far-eastern city with a severe power shortage. "Decorated with scattered lights, it was like a night at a fishing village." This remark happened to point out the origin of the city. As an unprofessional piano teacher, a connoisseur of small wontons, a beloved concubine of a playboy and a boarding student of a missionary school with deep affection for automobiles forty years ago, she would teach Xiang An her life experience every time they met. The boring inculcation was as harmful as her rigid piano finger exercises; nevertheless her voice was bright and crisp like the sound of a tramcar. When it came to the secrets of women, she would suddenly become as shy as a sister on stage, though all her lines were neatly-phrased, well-practiced and accomplished. The person she appreciated most was Xiang An's boyfriend, Luo Ke. "A handsome guy." By "handsome" she was referring to "lanky" in the soft southern dialect. Luo Ke looked bandy-legged from the back. He liked to wear terribly thick acrylic socks and skinny jeans with a stonewashed seat, which often gave others an impression of poor hygiene. "He is articulate and fond of books, a good young man with deep emotions," Xiang An's aunt commented. (What Luo Ke repeatedly related to others was Saul Bellow's Humboldt chasing a woman all around the room and shouting, "I'm a poet and I have a big penis.") Xiang An was also a charming and agreeable woman, with her Sartre-like eyes—it was no exaggeration to say that she was a wall-eyed woman who felt good about herself. She could use the left eye to stare at you and the right eye to glimpse at your left side. She would look very thoughtful as if she had just discovered another self of you standing right there. That said, Xiang An was still a beauty indeed. At night, when the city was noisy and crowded, the yellow-brown light from the iodine tungsten lamps would vaguely outline her petite and tight body. She was always energetic in darkness, which was fully appreciated by Luo Ke's mother. It would only be a few years before someone passing the station saw her waiting for the bus in the soughing wind with her legs exposed under the light grey coat (of course she was wearing flesh-colored stockings), and thought that her haggard look despite the heavy makeup must have been caused by Luo Ke. His incumbent girlfriend, the potential daughter-in-law, the future mother-in-law, was nothing like Luo Ke's amiable mother.

Fifty years ago, Luo Ke's mother could be regarded as a modern female. When she was young, she was as stubborn and rebellious as her son. She bobbed her hair (which was, however, unlike Luo Ke), read *New Youth*, went to the theatre filled with wooden stools to watch modern plays (in which her compatriots dressed up as westerners were standing on a place two feet above ground, pressing for a divorce), and ate snacks on the street by herself or in groups—a completely perverse appearance. But unexpectedly, she remained unmarried, waiting for her Mr. Right for a long time instead of running away from home, until the sophisticated Luo Yizhi captured her heart by his flow of play lines. There was no romance whatsoever in her premarital history, as a discolored and fragile photo covered with brown stains, the people in which were beyond recognition or long dead due to wars, diseases, accidents or mental sufferings. Their withered, small-sized souls floated to the depths of the universe and never looked back. The resolute mother once commented on a classmate who drowned herself in a river: she had a problem with her life.

Compared with Luo Ke's strong-willed mother, his paternal relatives were all good-for-nothings. His uncle, his father's unrestrained brother, who proclaimed himself a doctoral student at Cambridge in a letter home, died in a brothel in east London forty-five years ago, holding the golden bracelet of Luo Ke's rustic grandfather. The name of this brothel could be learned from a one-act play of the romanticist's playwright brother. Of course it was only a transliteration.

Luo Yizhi shot to fame with that play which strongly denounced capitalism. The famous play had only been performed twice in Luo Yizhi's play-writing career, which lasted half a century. In the latter half of the century, Luo Ke keenly expected for his father's sake that the play would be staged again or be adapted for TV and broadcasted sometime in the afternoon on the second drama channel. The infamous play, full of censure and enjoy a small group of audience, was called *On the Collapse of the Old Imperialism: from the Destruction of a Teenager from the Countryside*. It was once cited as *The Destruction of a Teenager and Collapse of Ism* by someone with an ulterior motive. The public called it *The Teenager from the Countryside*, and the insiders referred to it as *Teenager Destroyed Imperialism* for short.

6

Finally, Luo Ke, the mourner, pushed away the paper and pen in great disappointment, and staggered back to his bed. He decided to take a nap first, and after that, he would think about what had happened. He started to feel glad that he gave up the stupid idea of writing a letter in remembrance. It was rather absurd to write a letter to a dead person. Suddenly, Luo Ke realized he had intended to write the letter to Yin Mang's husband. "Hell, was I going to confide in that dwarf? The guy is nicknamed 'bantam.' Isn't the death of her wife's body his most ardent and enduring wish?" Luo Ke lay on the Taiwanese bamboo mat and swung his arms and legs for a while, celebrating his wise change of mind.

Yin Mang's husband, Sun Shu, was the most outstanding poor student Luo Ke had ever seen. For all his short stature and plain looks, he married a beauty. He was such a learned man that all the words of wisdom would spill over from his throat the moment he opened his mouth. He connected everything in the world in a unique way—Nietzsche, Nixon, Nicholas II, Nigeria, Nineveh, Nissan police cars—showing his knowledge with his silver tongue. It was enjoyable to listen to his speeches, of which the cadence in a theatrical manner reminded his listeners of a sulky doorman at a madhouse, or a braying mule in heat. His figure and looks were a kind of synthesis, the formula of which included: an elderly poet, a cold-shouldered football team substitute, a thug with unfulfilled ambitions, and a chattering artificer. In a nutshell, it would be very hard to find a member of the elite like him in the world now. According to himself, when he met Yin Mang, he was in the most difficult, distressful, critical situation of his life. (It was only later that Yin Mang learnt that this kind of situation would come any minute and almost became a routine.) All he could think about was suicide. Sylvia Plath's poem *Lady Lazarus* was popular at the time. All kinds of translations were circulated among all kinds of sentimental men and women. Enthusiasm for death and enthusiasm for talking about death merged into one. Hughes' attractive wife flurried the young generation. "Suicidal impulse," and "self," "self-love," "self-mutilation," "self-abasement," and even "self-contradiction," "self-satisfaction," "self-glorification," "self-elevation" and "self-abandon" became the pet phrases of young men and women. When Yin Mang's husband strolled out of the dirty gate of whatever school, at first glance there seemed to be only one man, but in fact, there were two miserable selves walking along. It was an age of the cult of appearance, and dark circles under the eyes, disheveled hair and a dirty face were considered the appearance of profundity. Though their relationship moved forward in a melancholic atmosphere and critical moments kept befalling him, his legs were as flexible as those of a martial arts athlete, and it was the energetic way he rode his bike that won Yin Mang's heart, plus of course whipping his bare back with the two-finger-wide belt in a locked bathroom in a moment of jealousy, as well as the indispensable clamor of death.

Luo Ke felt something had given him a press in the dream, and smiled in an inexplicable way. "You are a complete mental. You think you are Mona Lisa?" Xiang An's angry tone told him that she felt overly neglected. "What do we eat for dinner? Your mysterious smile?" Xiang An was annoyed and announced the hunger of her stomach and the grievance of her heart with a shrill voice. "If you shout again, I'll bump my head to death." Luo Ke suddenly felt how soothing it was to recite lines. "It surprises me that you should be so overwhelmed with sorrow," Xiang An said in a gentle voice, which added to Luo Ke's confusion.

Luo Ke wobbled off the bed and, imitating a sleepwalker's gait, zigzagged his way to the desk. He picked up the *Baudelaire* off the floor, closed the brick-like book and hit his head with it, as if he wanted to wake himself up. He put one hand on the stomach, and mumbled, "If we are hungry, we'll eat. As for what to eat, let's take a look at the fridge."

The honeymoon-like day drew to a close with a summer shower and emotional turmoil. No matter what they ate for dinner, they must say goodbye to this room and left the bed of the retired playwright. In several hours, Luo Yizhi would resume his endless pacing back and forth in this room and his tireless criticism of everyone except himself. And Luo Ke would always take the brunt. Therefore, they needed to suppress the impulse to recollect and the desire to quarrel, and to have some good food to comfort their miserable stomach and soul, storing the twenty-four hours of happiness and unhappiness as a catalyst for bad moods and materials for future squabbling.

It was a moonless night. The singing of Stefano, the passionate son of Italy, emanated from the window upstairs, expressing his yearning for the lover on a microgroove record. At the same time, there was a follower's voice with a similar volume but much weaker in expression. The follower paused now and then, making an effort to clear his throat, and then burst out on a high note with his awkward Italian to keep up with the deceased Stefano. "Pathetic bel canto. It would be perfect for the great tenor upstairs to act in Puccini's tragic operas, with his shouts and shrieks and desperate struggles." Luo Ke opened the door and listened to the voice of Stefano and its shadow rolling down from the staircase for a while. "That was an unlucky tenor accusing the summer heat. Just wait." Luo Ke said to Xiang An on his side, "When he finished practicing, he would ask his wife and children to do the dishes and take out the trash in his resonant voice."

Xiang An leant close against Luo Ke and remained still, listening to his boring sarcasm. Outside the round window above the turn of the stairs, there was a clump of oleanders planted against the wall. The scene of them being battered by the wind and rain was in harmony with the derelict fence a meter away. The lawn was soaked and muddy, and the smell in the air suggested the end of the shower. The night might be fresh and cool, but the following innumerable days seemed increasingly unpredictable. Walking leisurely on an avenue with a pram was purely a vision of giving birth, and the agony of the opening in the pelvis was almost in sight. Xiang An thought she would regret bitterly if she let Luo Ke create a life that was connected to her. The scorching summer was going away and autumn was coming, and the pleasant feelings brought by the change of season confirmed her in the thought. Xiang An ardently wrapped her arms around Luo Ke. "I love him, but he's not the one."

7

That winter passed away long ago, but still remained fresh in memory. The first snow of the winter lasted four hours, and had completely covered the dirty city by around seven o'clock in the evening. Every snowflake stood for a kind of purity that was easy to melt away. The next day, as long as the temperature permitted, another kind of transparent crystals that made pedestrians tremble with fear, would coldly replace the poetic scene of the night before. Luo Ke, a sloppy man, rode his Flying Pigeon bike with a broken back brake as fast as he could to meet Yin Mang. This muddleheaded yet talented woman from a prestigious university spent the day of their appointment in her poky room snacking on sunflower seeds with a hot water bottle in her arms, except when called out by other family members to take phone calls. It was December, and she had just come back from Beijing the day before.

It was Yin Mang's big brother that opened the door for Luo Ke. The small guy with sparse whiskers in his early forties kept staring at Luo Ke, baffled, until he knocked on Yin Mang's door and dodged in. When Luo Ke passed the living room, Yin Mang's seventh elder brother, who was sitting against the door, blocked the way. The famous cellist with a crew cut was performing Vivaldi in a very artistic way. "Make way there." It was only when his step mother appealed to him for the second time that this talented string music student of a music conservatory, who needed others to write essays for him, unabashedly put down the brown-haired bow and kicked the chair behind himself with one leg. "You are the fourth man that has come to visit her daughter today," introduced the musician, and then categorically pointed out, "You should have wiped your feet before you got in." "Sorry," Luo Ke explained in a gentle voice, brushing the snow off his coat above the cello, "I should have brought my slippers."

Since then Luo Ke had never visited this big, nursery-like family again, though from this united yet also sometimes disintegrated group that once had one father, three mothers and thirteen children, he managed to take the young Yin Mang away.

It was at the memorial service of Yin Mang's father that Luo Ke first met Yin Mang in this world of unpredictable meetings and partings. In the hall where the solemn funeral music reverberated, unlike any of her half-siblings with various characteristics, she seemed to be the only one untouched by the sounds of crying. She stood farthest away from her mother, as indifferent as a staff member of the funeral parlor. Luo Ke said to her later, "Silence in sufferings composes your most beautiful portrait." Yin Mang was younger than all her half-siblings. She was the only child of her father's third marriage. Her birth put an end to his ambitious plan of reproduction. Yin Dongshan was the most serious old man Luo Ke had ever met. His downward eyebrows, slightly closed eyes and pressed lips left an impression of misery. He was at the top of the hierarchy of this big family, but his pedigree and authority did not make him inapproachable. Yin Dongshan's favorite diversion was raising his arm and shouting "Fall in!" on a whim in his room.

8

Because of Yin Mang, the once unrestrained Luo Ke became self-disciplined. Winter in the south was cold and damp. After wandering on the streets for several nights, they had to end the loitering caused by the feverish love. On another snowy night, they slept together in Luo Ke's camp bed, with their bodies held on tightly, and opened up a new chapter in their life of perplexity.

Before this long and mysterious night, both of them were confined to a conceptual world of imagination which had been talked about by people for countless times. They had touched the skin of the opposite sex by courage and instinct. They had awakened and been awakened by others. But at that night, they experienced a flight, a permeating breath, and the first and also the last awakening. They made each other feel the only existence and the only being, after which they were confirmed that one could be completely oblivious of oneself. Many years afterwards, they were still steeped in the memory of that snowy night. All the pleasures at midnight or dawn were an echo to that night of eternity.

The moment Luo Ke tucked a loose strand of Yin Mang's black hair behind her ear, he inadvertently opened the door to desire. The night in the south with whirling snowflakes could be identified as a distinct part of their inner confession. When Yin Mang fully exposed her body to him, he was far more surprised than happy. In the pleasant dizziness, his imploration towards his own body surpassed the outward desire, and the stationary appealer seemed to be silently responding to his imploration.

Attracted by such singular serenity, they did not speak a word in the dimly-lit room, and outside the window, the snow scene was replaced by thousands of pigeons flapping their wings. The oil painting on the wall at the other end of the room depicted a river ready to overflow its bank, on which a solitary stone hut seemed to be waiting for the wind of felicity. On the edge of the white ceramic bowl hung a colorless drop of water, which seemed like a vestige of a splash, and the possibility of its dropping involved the prospect of bursting. The ticktack of the travel alarm clock with a faux leather surface was like the continuous sobbing of time. They could not find any sign of passion on each other's face. They held their hands tightly and looked down at this inexplicable gesture. Staring at each other inquiringly, they detected the smile in the move of their lips that praised kissing. For the first time he felt that resistance was an expression of invitation, an explanation of feeling at home. He smelled a long-anticipated, unfamiliar fragrance on her bright red tongue tip. When the sucking was suddenly encouraged by her teeth, they clearly felt the appeal of sexual desire, which was complemented by the wind and snow with a cold burning feeling. They paused in a breath, looking for the remaining desire on each other's lips as the evidence of their emotions. Lyric lines only crossed his mind with their rhythm and rhyme but a melody echoed in the air like an auxiliary note. The first knuckle of her index finger moved from the love and life lines in his palm to the inside of his wrist arteries, and then to the sentimental pores on his arm.

Her continual whispering became faster, and the words were indiscernible. Moaning was replaced by indistinct sobbing at times. She kept repeating some simple syllables to reveal the open secret. Sometimes, she held her breath and waited for his response to the only secret. In the most passionate dream they were unashamedly united like deities, and it encouraged their limitless exploration. The river of time shifted in the direction of the gentle and fertile plains by a slope, and the silt it carried along would form a deposit in the estuary, waiting under the water till the day of its surfacing and naming. It was like the gratitude of a virgin, and the first vow of fidelity.

Among the moments of meditation, small acts of disobedience and the following explicit consent, Luo Ke gained brilliance in his soul. In the meanwhile, the intoxication and the urge to leave turned his attention to the fatigue of his body. The shuttle of comfort connected his euphoria and lingering frustration. He wondered if it could be that the ultimate satisfaction equaled the ultimate boredom.

This was the moment they fell in love with each other; the folding bed kept creaking as if calling the wandering ghosts lost in the windy and snowy night, while Luo Ke and Yin Mang seemed eager to sink into oblivion in this age, with the temporary delirium of their bodies leading to the eternal loss of their souls. "Is this what you have long waited for?" Luo Ke gazed at Yin Mang in his arm, the other hand caressing both sides of her nose strewn by freckles. "I don't know. But I'll pray that such a night could happen again in my life. I'll be looking forward to it. Before tonight … I don't know. It might hurt you, but you might want to hear my true feelings. Before tonight, the man I was somehow infatuated with had nothing to do with you. But now, at this moment … " "It seems that I have been waiting for you all the time. It doesn't mean that I was familiar with you, but that it was the strangeness, you know? What you need is a stranger that you suddenly spot in a crowd. Do you really think that you need something you are familiar with?" "There is some difference. I think I'll be missing you after this, when we grow distant. It is fascinating to see someone you know gradually changing beyond recognition." "I think it's hard for me to stand such parting." "Do you think that these things only happen beyond the range of marriages?" Luo Ke fell silent. His excitement drained away. He saw his heartfelt words covered by ice and snow in an instant. His eyes narrowed, scrutinizing again this enchanting woman and their unforgettable night. According to Luo Ke's own standard, Yin Mang belonged to the kind of young woman that were thin but well-developed. Her skin was pale with a little color, nothing to elicit improper thoughts. But Luo Ke knew that it was because he was too young. She was a sensitive, paranoid, equivocal woman with unfathomable looks, and her leading Luo Ke, the unfortunate fellow, in the journey of life could indeed be reflected in a playful painting worth collecting. Spending the rest of the night chatting casually with legs wrapped around the hip after the sexual frenzy was only Luo Ke's imagination. Growing drowsy, both the observer and the observed lost their interest. Outside, the wind dropped and the snow ceased, along with which the window lattice lost its shock and impulse, and stopped vibrating in darkness. At dawn they fell asleep and plunged into dreams after their first night, which Luo Ke would put into his private record. The two sweaty bodies faced each other, and after a while, turned over, relaxed and even disappeared. They would never be further away from the world.

9

That night, when Luo Ke and Yin Mang plunged into the pitch-dark corridor on the ground floor, stamping and yawning. Luo Ke's pocket was caught by the bike at the corner. He blurted out a cuss word without disguise. Yin Mang did not comment, silently following him upstairs. It seemed that Luo Ke wanted to give a reasonable explanation, though as a result, he went even further by cursing a blue streak with complicated structure and selected expressions and did not stop even when they entered the house. Yin Mang looked at him thoughtfully, and understandingly bit her tongue. Not until their passionate first night did Yin Mang indirectly respond to his swearing half an hour ago. Seeming to add a piece of verbal tattoo on the body totem, she spoke in a soft voice on his side about medical research findings in America, "Clinical observation shows that when a man reaches orgasm, his IQ is as low as a dog's—zero."

Romantically panting, Luo Ke felt as if he had been slapped in the face, and exasperatedly held back his heartfelt words. He had intended to tell Yin Mang his feelings after their hot sex when it was still fresh in mind. The disjointed murmuring could have been both an aftertaste and a bewitching confession of love. But after Yin Mang's scientific quote, Luo Ke only said "I'm tired" and went straight to sleep.

The next morning, it was not until the warm sunshine had lit the most part of the bed that Yin Mang woke up from her messy dreams with cold hands and feet. Luo Ke, with his long limbs, had to twist his body on the narrow bed, like an abandoned orphan. His scruffy hair spread on the quilt, face buried in the pillow. It seemed that he would not get up before two o'clock in the afternoon. Yin Mang finally started looking around this small room less than ten square meters. There was nothing but the narrow bed they were lying on and the long table by the window. On the khaki wall hung a still life painting of the van Gogh style and some bright-colored pictures cut from pictorials or calendars to cover the stains. A pot of asparagus fern was placed on the windowsill, looking half-dead. Most noticeably, on the table there were eight or nine empty bottles surrounding a wine glass in a semi-circle like planets around the sun. Outside this flat solar system with a strong smell were some ballpoint pens and paper scraps, on one of which there was a poem. Luo Ke did not know where he got it (even maybe he himself composed it). He had planned to present it to Yin Mang on this special night. Now she was holding the scrap in her hand, trying to understand the profound meaning of the simple words—"The basket is your family crest, and I am another basket of yours." The crooked characters were packed tightly together and looked like the Arabic, which even evoked the picture of the poor Luo Ke dragging his pen on the paper when he struggled to write down the words. Painful helplessness and private self-admiration were combined in these grotesque Chinese characters that transcended the long history of handwriting. Right after these great yet badly written Chinese characters there was a smooth and cursive line of English. Yin Mang read out the words: Fälön, Sweden. She did not have the slightest intention of conjecturing the story behind the address. Her thoughts were directed to another man by the comparison of language. Sun Shu, a man with a strange tongue and nerve system, was an outstanding linguistic genius that had achieved remarkable accomplishments in spoken English. He spoke rhythmically, proficient in voiceless and voiced consonants, plosives and incomplete plosives, the American liaison, the Chicago slang and Shakespearean English, which was not all but had already led to Yin Mang's astonishment and admiration. But this southern maverick language genius had a little weakness. It seemed to the inarticulate Yin Mang that the poor man was never able to tell the retroflex sounds from cacuminal sounds in Mandarin Chinese, let alone the cruel front and back nasals. He talked with foreigners in mandarin with mixed accents (at those times he had to give up the southern dialect that he was greatly attached to), which easily blended into the mumbling of the foreigners who had just begun to learn Chinese. He completely fit in with them, and it made him feel a rare kind of ease to speak without differentiating between the four tones. When fraternizing with foreigners, Sun Shu, with his innate potential for discrimination, managed to conceal the slightest trace and behave in a natural and appropriate way. Yin Mang realized that she was comparing Sun Shu with Luo Ke, and thought that they did have something in common— outward arrogance and inward self-pity. The two young fellows living in the same clamorous era started to show their gallantry towards Yin Mang, a wily bluestocking, almost at the same time. Yin Mang basked in the winter sunshine so that her mind could wander comfortably. She wondered how she could remain so leisurely and turn a deaf ear to all the noises from the corridor outside. Luo Ke's father was squabbling with his wife over whether he should go to the nearby hospital to have an injection to reduce fever. Yin Mang listened for quite a while, and still couldn't figure out who wanted to go out and who was opposing it. After a while, things quieted down and it seemed that the couple had gone out together. Compared with Yin Mang's bazaar-like family life, such fluctuating tumult only belonged to a tranquil small town. The family under Yin Dongshan's domination was a miniature of New York. His Marxism and Yin Mang's existentialist remarks from Sartre's plays coexisted; her big brother's yogi-like taciturnity and her seventh brother's endless classical music perfectly complemented each other; music kept going on due to Yin Dongshan's third wife's preference for Suzhou Pingtan (an art performance); his twelfth daughter was always on the phone, filling the big busy house with her inquires, greetings, goodbyes of all styles and exaggerated reactions towards some bad or good news. Yin Mang's twelfth sister, the volunteer telephone operator, was the most incredible one in this bewildering melting pot. She was originally a nurse in a community hospital, then somehow became a secretary in a joint venture of toy manufacturing, and ended up, unfortunately and incredibly, being arrested for hooliganism because she was involved with a black man of unknown identity and nationality. Yin Mang always called her "Little Sister," which almost replaced her name.

Due to movement of the celestial bodies, the pale winter sunlight receded from the room. The bright Yin Mang was suffering from cold and hunger. "Get up." She had to wake up the lazy slave. When Luo Ke was in bed, he would rather take care of his limbs than his stomach, which was always willing to fulfill its duty. When he was sitting at the table, it would be a different story. The gourmet in imagination, yet an idler in real life, was now in a stupor, half awake. Freud, the Austrian psychiatrist, and his bitter opponents were fighting over his will, torturing his confused mind on the saw between id and superego. Luo Ke's soul was lingering between consciousness and subconsciousness. He was always driven out of a gentle dream by anxiety, and in the realm of consciousness, he was a fidgety painter, brandishing the brush in his heart and scrawling on a wilderness without any depth of field. The colorful strokes of desire formed a bewildering scene including ghosts and monsters that Luo Ke himself did not recognize, his beloved relatives and friends in disguise, and several well-dressed couples he had never met who were dancing ceaselessly ... In other stupefying dreams, according to his fragmentary flashbacks, he was an eloquent talker. Usually in those glorious moments, Luo Ke would witness groups of glib giants and dwarfs defeated by his flowing words and kneel in shame. Then he was intoxicated by the haunting fragrance at night and his soul floated out of his body. In a trance, Luo Ke, wretchedly all alone, tumbled onto a wobbly canoe and hurriedly set off for the River Lethe in Dante's work. The fire of the inferno was burning in the distance, and the Sword of Damocles was hanging above. At this life-or-death moment, the savior Yin Mang pinched him with perfect timing and waked him up. "You were having a dream," Yin Mang told the dreamer Luo Ke. "Yes," admitted the bleary-eyed Luo Ke, "a very banal dream." He thought to himself that it must be the affluent ladies and gentlemen of the leisure class like Jung that blocked the sewers of dream and deprived the spiritually poor like him of the chance of a decent dream. "The monumental works of psychoanalysis made dreams a set of concepts and terms." The sleepyhead Luo Ke thought it was true, at least for him. Another true predicament was that there was a chill in the room. This small room that accompanied Luo Ke day and night was only for the housemaid in the architect's design. Downstairs, the dentist also set up a plank bed on the bathtub in his bathroom, where his eldest son had endless nightmares or woke up with a start after falling asleep.

"Touch me," muttered Yin Mang, cuddling against Luo Ke, like a bird perching in the tree which fluffed its feathers in a cold wind. She pointed at her rounded nose tip. Luo Ke gently touched it in a calm manner. "A dog's nose," he commented objectively, "icy cold." The brief remark triggered a new round of pleasures.

10

Whether strolling in the crowded street or curling up in bed for the remaining heat, Luo Ke was completely unaware of the surrounding danger. In an era full of conspiracies and lowdown, there was no more of the so-called private life. Luo Ke thought it was an era without privacy, as if people were living in a transparent tube. Therefore he was always patiently waiting for misfortunes, such as stumbling on his shoelace right after going out, the bike bell being half removed, the dirty stiff handkerchief stolen on a bus, sand getting into eyes, and being injected with estrogen by a nurse after the circumcision, etc. An imminent danger was that he forgot it was the last Sunday of December.

Liu Yazhi, an art teacher of a suburban elementary school, a fan of Luo Yizhi's plays, a victim of a broken marriage, an all-rounder in kitchen, a charming 39-year-old woman, and a free model for photo shoots with a lifelong commitment, was now walking in high spirits to the meeting place which provided a bit of warmth to the lonely and long life. It was the familiar three-storied villa where Luo Ke's single bed was located. After taking a bus and a trolleybus, and then another trolleybus and another bus, she arrived. In her delicate blue canvas handbag there was a Konica Z-up 80—it cost her a fortune to buy this brand-name camera, which made her feel uneasy for quite a while. Liu Yazhi, with a small head, liked being photographed with all her heart. She had been extremely happy since she met Luo Ke, an amateur photographer who liked to toot his own horn. Every time she saw Luo Ke narrowing his loving right eye behind the camera, mumbling compliments like "good," "great," "excellent" and "gorgeous," she could not help beaming. And after a shower of compliments, it took ten to twenty minutes for the shutter button to be reluctantly pressed. Her neck, elbows, waist, knees and all the other important flexible body parts were crying with ache. Nevertheless, Liu Yazhi, who had enough confidence in her looks, still enjoyed the process.

The relationship could be traced back to the time when Liu Yazhi was a cautious patient of the dentist Zhang Rongtian. Her left front tooth was hit off by her ex-husband, who was practicing like an amateur boxer at home, and swallowed down. Her ex-husband, a PE teacher at the same school with her, took the trouble to guard the hospital gate, preventing his poor wife from wearing a false tooth, and spread the word that he would humiliate her. In the time of helplessness, Liu Yazhi, injured and insulted, was sent to Zhang Rongtian's private clinic by fate.

Zhang Rongtian, a filial son, went to visit the grave of his long-deceased mother in the Suzhou (Jiangsu Province) countryside, hence the empty house and the closed door. Liu Yazhi, desperate and having no clue about what happened, rang the three doorbells one by one outside the villa and kept waiting. She felt like crying after repeated ringing, which woke up Luo Ke, who was lying in. He had just finished his military service and was idly waiting at home for an assigned job. He received the stubborn patient in his own room. Liu Yazhi, after a good cry, told Luo Ke about her miserable marriage with the hissing sound of a snake, regardless of whether he liked it or not. By extension, she advised her listener against committing the mistake of stepping into the dreadful trap of marriage after informing him of the whereabouts of her front tooth. After that, she came to the clinic several times, and every time she finished a session of clinical treatment of her front tooth, she would come upstairs to sit awhile with Luo Ke. Having nothing to do, Luo Ke properly played the role of an amiable, sincere and patient listener. When Liu Yazhi became cool about her uncomfortable false tooth, she was already sitting at the table in Luo Yizhi's house, talking cheerfully about her favorite flavor of toothpaste.

For a long time afterwards, they talked pleasantly, made

harmless jokes about themselves and each other, until things changed in an odd moment of an afternoon. They talked about camera filters for a while, and suddenly felt there was nothing to say. In silence, they had a hunch about the gravity of the matter and saw the beginning of what was going to happen. "I had a divorce." Suddenly Liu Yazhi told him the fact that had existed for half a year. It was not the divorce itself, but the appropriate statement of it that changed their relationship, which had not shown the slightest sign before, like a paper knife cutting a piece of blank paper. Luo Ke always regarded a sharp blade as a symbol of fate. It made things perish and cut things open to expose the unavoidable internals.

A pot of asparagus fern appeared on the windowsill in Luo Ke's room, an unnoticeable gift from Liu Yazhi. A little water and sunshine and the cool environment allowed it to continue the slow growth, which had begun long ago.

"Hey," Yin Mang gently complained in his ear, "you are not attentive enough. Don't tell me it's your thing." "It's my lot," Luo Ke said to himself.

The snow in the middle of the street had completely melted, and several boys wearing brightly colored stocking caps were trampling on the snow on the pavement back and forth for fun. They breathed the clean air rare for this city with ruddy faces, and shrieked from time to time as if they were calling others' attention to their lighthearted game.

In this world of numerous doctrines and lurking dangers, the elusive relationship between an unfortunate man and an unfortunate woman was determined the moment they met. Maybe it was like a video game, with its dazzling colors and the tricky preset program. As soon as one plugged it into the power of desire, pressed the button of sensibility and swung the gamepad of sense, the lone warrior of love would hopelessly charge toward failure again and again. The romantic Luo Ke was just such an intrepid warrior. When Liu Yazhi had her new bright tooth fixed, the son of the retired playwright was writing his first short novel about how a masculine boy dumbly fell in love with an innocent girl. Luo Ke was jittery to let Liu Yazhi read the first and the only two pages. She complimented on his writing, and then strongly advised the embryonic novelist with a good literary background to rid himself of the fancy idea. She thought someone like Luo Ke, whose enthusiasm could only last five minutes, was not suitable for such stupid and extremely tedious work which would lead to hemorrhoids. Luo Ke argued that an American writer (Hemingway, who once served in the army, he thought to himself) wrote while standing. "Then he must have had ulcers on the soles of his feet." Her ruthless posture temporarily ended Luo Ke's writing dream.

The middle aged Liu Yazhi told her junior Luo Ke that a young man should go out of his room and get to know the constantly changing world instead of staying at home and being indulged in fantasies as if he were sick. In fact, Luo Ke, who was sick of himself, went out of his room and stepped into Liu Yazhi's room.

Then came the time when they could not bear to part from each other. Though Luo Ke secretly gave up Hemingway and turned to imitating Calvino—writing about a horse split in two by an evil man, he was taken as Liu Yazhi's art student on the surface. Of course, what he learned for free was not just the relationships between colors and the expressive power of lines. In Liu Yazhi's room stuffed with albums of painting masters and anonymous reproductions. Luo Ke, with his agile mind, soon became a trained artisan who could make a canvas so brightly colored that it became tacky. The retired serviceman waiting for a desirable job went to work at a cinema near Liu Yazhi's school through her wholehearted recommendation. He was paid for drawing a poster for the upcoming movie every week. It was half a year or so before Luo Ke, the criticized poster painter, was politely kicked out of the cinema, as the residents nearby unanimously complained that the cinema had been playing feature movies starring repulsive-looking people in the recent six months, which was, of course, just based on the posters. Luo Ke retired again. Only this time, from the interface between the movie industry and art, he went into the realm where applied art and the enamelware industry converged—a downtown department store, still benefited from Liu Yazhi's recommendation, his first painting teacher. Luo Ke's first assignment was to paint a row of ten long-stemmed spittoons (twelve if space permitted) with various patterns on a piece of stiff paper to decorate the shop window.

After nearly a year's careful observation, though Liu Yazhi could not conclude that Luo Ke, who liked gaudy colors, was weak-sighted or color blind, she was sure that he was gifted in wasting (not only pigments). He was long-haired or bald, and looked uninhibited and successful with hands in his pockets. He was once deeply touched by Irving Stone's *Lust for Life*, not because he admired van Gogh's talent or felt sorry for his tough life, but because Theo's lifelong financial help offered to artists made him moan over his desolation as an only son.

11

What also needed moaning was the fleeting time and Liu Yazhi, who was walking fast. At the speed of an emergency muster, Luo Ke transformed himself from an idler in bed into a panicky man wrapped in his overcoat. Impelled by his inexplicably fast speed, Yin Mang also threw on her clothes, "What's wrong?" Luo Ke looked at Yin Mang with her uncombed hair and regretted. He thought it was wrong to deceive the woman he was madly in love with, and on a whim, he decided to rectify his mistake by telling her everything in order to obtain the forgiveness of Yin Mang, who was well educated and reasonable.

The doorbell in the corridor menacingly went off. Luo Ke could almost see the stubborn Liu Yazhi still pressing the black button hard with her finger.

Zhang Rongtian, the dentist, played role of the god of fate

this Sunday noon. An earth-shaking bang came from the ground floor. His son rushed out of the door with shrieks and headed into the freezing world of December without looking back. The door wide open, the dentist in his late fifties, shivering in the draft, cursed his unfilial offspring in tears and swore to heaven that he would remove every last one of his son's thirty-two teeth.

Liu Yazhi, as someone who fully appreciated family tragedies, felt it obligatory to comfort the widower standing in the cold draft. She assisted him back into the house and helped him to ease the rage as a former patient. In the meanwhile, Luo Ke, who was on the brink of catastrophe, took advantage of the old man's distress. He stealthily led the confused Yin Mang downstairs and hurried out after the dentist's son, which avoided the folly of introducing one woman to another. At the same time, he rang the death knell for Luo Ke's seemingly immoral relationship with Liu Yazhi and seemingly unobjectionable relationship with Yin Mang.

12

Luo Ke, with his hair wet, was walking slowly in the drizzle. His arms were swinging back and forth, which seemed to match the splashes caused by his feet. Wherever he went, the passers-by were all avoiding him as if he were a watering cart coming straight towards them. The ill-tempered Luo Ke looked sullen at the moment, like a soldier patrolling in an occupied area.

He was on the way to Xiang An's house. The carnivore set off early in the morning in order to appear at the table on time. As it was a long journey, Luo Ke divided it into three laps in advance—twelve minutes of biking, then the No.27 tramcar to the terminus after leaving the bike in the alley near the station, and, now for the last, the final dash towards his lover and lunch across a village.

An erotic episode Luo Ke experienced in the tramcar must

be mentioned here. It was about nine o'clock in the morning, and the carriage was crowded as usual. Passengers from all over the country filled the damp carriage with a nasty fishy smell. Several groups of young women scattered around were broadcasting all kinds of private matters and hobbies in a loud voice that made Luo Ke feel drowsy. Suddenly, a handsome middle-aged man clasped him to his chest. Luo Ke squinted at him and almost fainted. The man, with a clean white face, opened his small mouth and showed Luo Ke his teeth covered by tartar. The smile gave off a pungent smell of pickles as if the pervert's stomach were being pumped right under Luo Ke's nose. Immediately Luo Ke was overwhelmed by the feelings of vomiting and diarrhea. With numb and cold limbs, he squeezed into the crowd, hoping to get rid of the tramcar freak. However, the bad breath always surrounded his neck tightly, with audacious persistence in making him faint.

Panicking, Luo Ke had to get off early. He then turned around and glared at the door, which clanged shut. Through the window, Luo Ke saw a face with an ingratiating smile bidding him goodbye. It suddenly occurred to him that he had met the guy somewhere, but the Proustian way of association did not help. He racked his brains with the clue of the bad breath only to recollect nothing related to the homosexual. He walked for quite a while in the rain, still unable to dispel the uneasiness. "I have to take a shower." The passing thought finally knocked open the door of memory. The scene in the summer swimming pool returned to Luo Ke's mind. "The dick of that bitch was really impressive."

For many years, wandering aimlessly on the street had been a major physical manifestation of Luo Ke's spiritual life. On countless gloomy afternoons and sunny mornings, Luo Ke, depressed, walked through vacant streets and alleys alone. He would often visit some hardware stores, which sold things like hinges and small scissors, hanging around the counter and browsing the newspapers and invoice books left by the salesmen.

Usually he would roam to a newly built road and sniff the smell of the asphalt several meters away. These might count as most of Luo Ke's leisure activities. He could have relived his old dreams on the third lap of the journey, but the appearance of the sophisticated sodomite made him have difficulty in urinating, let alone in dreaming of his romantic encounter with beautiful women walking in a hurry.

The unceasing autumn rain in the south was the garland of desire on this obscene morning. The shop windows along the pavement were covered with a cold mist. As if he had been raped just now, Luo Ke's facial expression was dramatic, features distorted by indignation and humiliation. Flashbacks of the episode in the tramcar constantly recurred to his mind, and the whole day was ruined.

13

The desktop recorder was playing a piano duo. The virtuosity slightly reduced the tackiness of the endless tenderness, while the arpeggio and the breathtaking moving sequence radiated the madness of cramming into a tramcar in rush hours. Xiang An, with a kind heart, was generally intoxicated by such emotional hallucinogens. Nothing was more pleasant than preparing lunch at home on a rainy morning, at least as far as Xiang An was concerned. From time to time she walked to the window, looked out at the gloomy sky, and then looked down to see if Luo Ke's tottering figure had appeared. Xiang An meticulously made it a point to change a cassette for the recorder in the intervals of her bustling around. This time it was a band fiddling with their inferior violins, creating a messy and piercing piece in unison, though the theme was still love.

Xiang An's father decorated their room as a simple hostel room in a fresh style, as if they would move away at any minute. In fact they had lived here for almost forty years. Now that Xiang

An's parents were absent, it became Xiang An's paradise she had long dreamed of. After Xiang An left her mother's womb, she came into the world, or this room, with whitewashed walls. Since she was out of the delivery room, she had slept in this room with her family every night until Luo Ke turned up.

Xiang An had been an enthusiastic and pure girl before she met Luo Ke the freak. Her innocent soul experienced the first shock on the playground in the middle school. A PE teacher, whose face was dotted with acnes, somehow got angry. He threw a volleyball at a girl student's bottom and yelled a swear word. Xiang An was petrified. She had never heard such a sonorous obscenity. It sowed the odd seeds of her sexual awareness. Luo Ke knew this. She would be ecstatic if he kept swearing when they were making love. He swore in whispers, as if nails were gently touching the skin, controlling the breathing of the nerves under.

She stayed in the empty room alone, as if watching over an African desert in rain. The humidity reminded her of every moment of desire. She was waiting for Luo Ke, desperately shouting as if she got lost in the luxuriant and moist jungle of thoughts. A crimson window opened in her heart chamber to welcome the storm of blood. The forceful beating passed on to every nerve and brought about nervous disorder and ecstasy. The inflated hot-air balloon in her body rose above the green grass, like a lost kite, a drunkard, an unsuccessful stammering speaker and the last five minutes of a movie footage. Some suffocating kind of love lingered around her. Her sentiment was like a hardly closed window, through which the ferocious wind and heavy rain ruthlessly rushed in. A slight chill soothingly penetrated into the skin, like the rheumatic pain into marrow. Subtle joy was rolling in the air, like a nebula surrounding a green planet in an astronomic photograph. She became a luminous body in her own imagination, rapidly spinning and sucking in dust of thoughts. The distant and lasting phenomenon of life in her knowledge was transformed into a shooting star and experienced by her in an instant. Sometimes, she was a mysterious and tranquil pasture where wind gently blew, while other times, she was an ambitious horsewoman and the horse that she knew well, the mane of her desire fluttering like flames. She breathed out heartfelt words and breathed in the sibling affection. Though with expectation and reverberation, her black pupils dilated indiscernibly, intruding into the white part. In the sweet and friendly fusion, they came to understand the lure of death, dispersedly pushed towards the world of unconsciousness and convulsively dropped into the journey in the mirror alone like an expected summary.

Just before twelve o'clock, Luo Ke appeared in the doorway like a soaked rooster, exasperated. Xiang An rushed to open the door and looked at him lovingly, with no idea how to attend to this aggressive rooster. Luo Ke pondered for quite a while outside the door as a rooster did, as if he were thinking whether he should get rid of his dripping feathers in the corridor. Xiang An, with her quick mind, readily understood the situation. When he was dissatisfied with one thing, he would become dissatisfied with everything. The best way to avoid Luo Ke's hostility against the whole world was to put him into clean clothes. To match Luo Ke's bad mood, Xiang An pretended to rummage through the wardrobe first, and then took out a neatly folded red acrylic tracksuit and poured hot water in a basin to let Luo Ke wash his hair and clean himself. "I have something to tell you." Xiang An poured water on Luo Ke's neck with a jade green plastic rinse cup while thinking how those critical game-changing lines were uttered in historical movies. "I've always wanted to talk to you about this." Luo Ke, who was rubbing his hair with a towel, suddenly grew nervous, as the librarian never prepared others for her subject. He stared at her for a while with water droplets clinging to his eyelashes. "You are pregnant." "Is this the greatest disaster you can imagine?" Xiang An herself did not know why she used the word disaster, though Luo Ke was completely terrified by this dangerous word. "You know that words could bring bad luck. Some are not to be casually used." Luo Ke tried to make her take back the "disaster" with an earnest reasoning.

Again, Xiang An hesitated, and after hesitating one more time, she swore on her miserable heart again that she would never tell Luo Ke that appalling story of incest.

They ate silently in the room, and then made love silently on the bed. When Luo Ke's breathing quickened like a rising tide, Xiang An saw that figure again. She came back to her girlhood in another vision, back to the last one of her countless visits to her only uncle, back to the attic with a triangular roof, back to her father's brother's arms.

On that night called the night, her uncle, abandoned by his wife for many years, was waiting for her under a fifteen-watt incandescent light bulb. The pharmacist working at a chest hospital looked like a delirious mourner on a funeral, his sad face full of lines of desire. The room was unusually clean, almost spotless. As usual, she pushed open the door, which was left ajar, and he was sitting upright on the well-polished floor beside the bed ...

Many years afterwards, on a day that Xiang An was nearly unable to recognize, her parents thought it was time to tell their daughter the truth, and took her to her uncle. They told her amiably that the man, who then lowered his eyelids, the uncle that she was obliged to visit once a week in her teenage years, the once miserable man abandoned by his wife, had given them his own daughter, as they themselves were unable to produce babies. And the girl was ... It was the movie that Xiang An most frequently played in her personal movie theatre. She completely understood Luo Ke's advice, knowing how words could bring misfortune. "Fine," Xiang An dejectedly said to herself in Luo Ke's arms, "just let me lie to him once."

14

In the memory as worth cherishing as the setting sun, and in the narration of an unknown year in the future, Luo Ke was a crying child under a magnolia tree. In the late autumn, his little figure stood on a lawn at dusk, comforted by the night breeze. The rivers, mountains and forests that were gradually growing distant symbolized the secrets in his heart. Their indifference in nature indicated some artificial things. The most tranquil streets, alleys in the cold wind of winter and the old apartments in his childhood memory suddenly changed their appearance, and became part of a lingering old story. Wandering in his imagination, Luo Ke kept rewriting a family fable, and turned its hidden sword of vengeance around. The narrator, who had no audience and was reluctant to learn, encouraged himself to write a book of fire. In a myriad of fiction, he encountered a Greek story of fate by chance. In ancient times when the noble sweet scent of bodies permeated, on the shore of the Aegean Sea, Oedipus approached his bloody doom in a pamphlet, speaking Chinese. With this, Luo Ke's crazy community story gained the horizon of scenery. He no longer made voyages, and started to wash off the unknown humiliation in the harbor of his heart.

In Luo Ke's view, gods and their children lived in the earthly world in ancient times. In their endless days, they went to temples, battlefields, palaces, city halls, streets, movie theatres, schools, and train stations, leaving their footprints everywhere. Their substitutes remained invisible around us. The gods saw through the conspiracy Luo Ke planned in his imagination, and ordered him to repay by flesh eternally. He tried to write an Oriental fable about loyalty in delirious ravings, but hatred diminished his power like opium. Disappointedly, he was merged with his story and remained in deep sleep for countless centuries.

His mother's mother, Luo Ke thought, asked her descendants to seek for the profound meaning of staying alive and express it in an elegant and wise language while living in fragments of time. He had experienced its appearance and ritual for innumerable times in dreams: a handful of corn under the pagoda tree, a bracelet beside a well, a piece of *suona* music in the bright sun, a ballad in the west wind, a pool of clear water in a yard, a literary name on a hanging scroll, a strand of grey hair by the candle light, and a sigh lingering among rivers and mountains. When he met the sophisticated Liu Yazhi in the season when southern magnolias quietly blossomed, Luo Ke immediately turned into a full-time dreamer, and it became more and more difficult for him to distinguish the blurred boundary between day and night. The complicated ways of the world was no doubt an impassable maze for him, who always stumbled while walking. Luo Ke adhered stubbornly to the thought that the attempt to get out of the maze was both futile and boring, and the essence was to get completely lost in it.

15

In the comprehensive maze of Liu Yazhi, Luo Ke first ventured into the maze of painting. As a natural enemy of plastic arts, he was very lucky to have fled in another way before reaching the dead end. What followed was the maze of women. Luo Ke, clumsy and stupid, over-optimistically went the wrong way and irrevocably headed towards the edge of a cliff where he would fail miserably. Liu Yazhi fully anticipated his doom. On a spring day when flowers bloomed and scented the air, Liu Yazhi invited Luo Ke to go on a walk in the warm breeze. They went through noisy streets and alleys, and made amateur comments on all kinds of bizarre constructions along the way. Liu Yazhi saw the bustling crowd as the common herd without exception, and disseminated absurd theories like "suffering accompanies you." Having passed numerous chaotic and desolate scenes, Liu Yazhi the strategist calmly took Luo Ke, the young fellow with a dry mouth and aching legs, to the depths of the maze. Proverbially, the winding path led to a secluded place. Confronted with a born winner, Luo Ke, with no idea of what to do, awkwardly fumbled here and there and finally came into Liu Yazhi's arms, flustered and surprised.

That was another intoxicating moment in Luo Ke's life. With the tireless prompting of Liu Yazhi, who had just got out of the crazy divorce proceedings, Luo Ke identified the sunny afternoon among many similarly colorless days. He talked with Liu Yazhi for a while on a slope in a secluded alley, immersed in the sweet and a little bit lifelessly serene atmosphere created by the cobble stone alley, the wrought iron gate, the half open shutters on a red brick wall, and the clean batik silk scarf hung outside a window for drying. They stood on the sunny side and recollected the preciously pleasant feelings when time seemed to have stopped, wiping their shoes against the gravel under the wall as if enjoying every second. Lost in thought, they stood there silently, looked at each other once in a while and smiled understandingly, radiating joy and contentedness. The two players, who itched to have a try before a friendly competition, were reluctant to leave the peaceful alley, as if they were killing time here. Luo Ke looked at the middle-aged woman in front of him and somehow pitied her. She gazed at him joyfully with a completely innocent look, legs crossed in the tweed dress. "She dressed too young for her age." Luo Ke did not dare to speak out, and then started his study and speculation about this mature woman.

Luo Ke romantically magnified their brief stay before Liu Yazhi's house, which made him feel that time started spinning rapidly after he came in. Liu Yazhi ran to a small square mirror, let down the bun on her head and shook her long hair. Obviously she had carefully washed and combed it in advance. Such pleasing tricks in the bedroom almost became part of her instincts, which completely surpassed the general meaning of making up before a mirror. The room was unusually dark, with double-layer curtains covering all windows. At the bedside, a tiny light installed on a flexible lamp-holder was producing a ghostly light, and the funeral atmosphere overwhelmed the desire that was going to be ignited. Liu Yazhi walked back and forth in the room in a composed manner, as light as a substitute warming up before entering the field. It seemed that in this quiet afternoon Luo Ke would save his young body and wake it up from ignorance. He lifted a corner of the velvet curtain and exposed his face in the afternoon sunshine. The scarlet curtain complemented his skin and created an illusion that his face were glowing. Five meters away was a house similar to Liu Yazhi's residence, most of its windows below the second floor shadowed by a huge phoenix tree. With a gentle slope, the alley turned east to a quiet street, bordered by black fences that had just been painted with tung oil. On the north side of the street was a ferry, while on the south was a section of the embankment outside the harbor district, exposed in front of the houses by the river. Lapped by waves, the uncovered embankment gradually grew barren and dismal. With black glints of sunshine on the muddy water, the river spoke the language of the lonely, floating things silently buried in the slow and relentless ebb and flow. Their physical state changed in order as from the sun, water to air, and under the indifferent and everlasting starry sky, they were transformed into vegetation and deposits on the land. Once they were a bubbly pool of blood but now there was nothing but stillness. On the opposite bank of the flurry and muddy river, a dock stood alone, exposing its rusty inside to the channel. The motionless scene reminded him of a bloody and brutal afternoon that stood out in his memory many times. In that afternoon of 1966—a paralyzed whole afternoon composed of sirens, Chinese *gongs* and drums, the nation's arm and the throat of descendants of the Yellow Emperor—Luo Ke witnessed the skeleton of his father's spirit and the weariness of his heart, which was as peaceful as crystal. On the day of surrender, which consisted of paper, ink, paste, groom, black, white, green, red, shouting and amplified shouting, Luo Yizhi, under the threat of a group of indignant intruders, kneeled right in front of his son, licking the blood stains on the floor with his bleeding tongue. The moment the soft tip of tongue licked the dark red bloodstains, the clamorous world slipped into a quiet crack. It was as if the violent soldiers in the house became nameless stone statues in a cavern, who were witnessing an episode of the revolution with the sacrificial indifference. Luo Ke tried to comprehend the meaning of tongue as the portal of life. It was a spoon in a cup, a piece of silverware to extract meaning and, at the same time, a fragrant body for sacrifice on an altar, charcoal in a fire, a dreamlike bouquet of flowers, an extension of sexual desire, or it was just the sexual impulse of the lower part of Luo Ke's body at the moment.

In a pause that seemed to have anaesthetized his breathing, Liu Yazhi came to Luo Ke's side. Before turning to her, Luo Ke tried his best to imagine her as a fecund treasure trove, a jellyfish in an aquarium, a dewdrop covered by leaves in a jungle and a mysterious cave he might and must go deep into. When he had completely turned around in his memory, he was pulled into a warm lake in astonishment, and Luo Ke thought this hug made him lose all the hugs he had had before. Inexplicably, a feeling between burning and flying was deeply embedded in his senses. In the long breaths connected together like fish scales, carnal desire filled his lungs like pollen, which made him crave for the arrival of a succession of wet kisses. In the meanwhile, his lust was like a sea gull, flying fast, watching and searching above the gentle water for a rescue call. His passion was dancing in his body, waiting for a hearty performance and the sensitive appreciation of it. He was looking forward to a dazzling conversation, a glittering mirage on the territory of skin.

Nevertheless, Luo Ke felt that the flight in flames was so lonely, absolute, winding, proud, and primitive that only the chanting of the motherland could match it and reveal its brilliant secrets.

They stopped, as if observing the remaining traces of a blasphemous carnival. They smoked cigarettes one after another, without talking or even making the slightest noise. Luo Ke gazed at her white, plump body like a peeper, and stroked her naked body again with sober eyes. He allowed a slight impulse to vibrate, and waited quietly for another chance to play that unfamiliar melody. He imagined of opening her private parts again and coming into where the uninterrupted flow of spring water came from. At the same time, he was daunted by a voice inside him. A kind of morality, which he could not describe, was menacing his lying body. He could almost see himself swallowed by the beautiful woman. He felt lucky that he was only a child, a big child, who had just joined an evil parade. Though he had barely reached the age to prove his sexual ability, he took the test of principles only after a few thoughts.

From afternoon to evening, Luo Ke was quietly searching and thinking back, as if there were something commemorative in the air. When night fell, the distant but distinct sound of waves lapping against the embankment came to his eardrums again, which reminded him of a woeful tune. Bending over, he watched the sleeping Liu Yazhi and comprehended a woman's plaints through gazing at the part between her neck and shoulder. She was resting her body, as well as her experience, in this dim room for a long time. By a mature woman, Luo Ke was overwhelmed by happy thoughts. His senses were controlled by the outside world and his ability to approach intelligence vanished. What he could barely approach in his brain was the tick-tock of the desk clock, which symbolized the loop of time—an illusion designed by humans to deceive themselves.

"You've slept for a long time," Luo Ke gently whispered in Liu Yazhi's ear, as if passing a secret message. The afternoon nap had aged her. Lines appeared around her eyes like folding fans, though they were extremely delicate as if made of sandalwood. Her eyes blinked, inducing Luo Ke's longing for the delicate fragrance.

"I'm a heavy sleeper. Did I talk in my sleep?" "No. The way you sleep seems like you intended it that way. You were smiling as if you were awake." "I always dream. I dream about sex. It calms me down. There are things I can't tell you ..." Liu Yazhi suddenly stopped, looking at Luo Ke. She did not know whether she was unwilling to, or just unable to tell her sensitive lover about that secret story. But Luo Ke's earnest eyes seemed to be calling for her retrospection, expressing his comfort and request. "If you feel it is hard to tell me, you can just imagine that you are talking to yourself. Of course, I'm another person to you, but I think everyone has some 'another person' apart from himself or herself." "Oh, when you talk like that, it makes others feel that you are a trap." "No, not me. It's what I say, my words …"

16

In the story that Liu Yazhi had repeated to herself for innumerable times, having a shower in summer was like adding milk into hot coffee, like excessive smoking and drinking. Another name of it was sexual impulse and delirium.

"Seventeen years old." I could not describe the age, the age that you could not know well or forget, and the age that you wanted to erase most. At that time you thought that you knew everything and instinctively grasped everything in the cosmos. It was the only and the last time that you transcended your life. At that age, you could create a new philosophy; you could hear the voice in your heart every day and night. Once past that age, you could never have that moment again. You even hoped to be raped. Of course, it was just hope, with no subject. You could never imagine how dangerous it was, and how carefree you were in that danger. At the age of seventeen, one was a sophisticated teenager, an ignorant little grown-up. It was an age of great intelligence. You could quickly distinguish all the things in your view, but remained completely ignorant of your own situation. One at that age belonged to an inner self, a mask without disguise in a diary, which made one dizzy …

Luo Ke thought the beautiful woman in front of him was walking around a mysterious center with a strong gravitational force. Her look indicated some irresolute longing, like an urgent letter carrying a purely personal revelation. Every move seemed hesitant, as if a swifter move would ignite the sparkles in the air. She remained silent in the dim room for a long time, almost self-oblivious, and seemed to be waiting for someone else to tell her story. Her skin, which had been caressed to maturity, gave a dark glow on Luo Ke's side like soft mud. It was beyond his imagination what kind of story was born inside this plump body. It might be as common as stone steps, which would, with every flight, lead to the highest place where one could look down at everything.

She finally started talking, her dreamlike voice floating in darkness like a sailboat at the mercy of wind. "I don't remember the exact date, probably someday in 1966 or 1967. It was summer, or maybe autumn. A typical humid day in the south. It doesn't matter. What matters is that I was less than seventeen years old. I remember my colored chalk, which I often used to draw animals and people on the chair rail. My mother always criticized me for that, as if I had been the chalk. She was a tidy woman, and almost had nothing to do but clean the dust off the furniture. She loved me as much as my father did. You can say that they spoiled me, and that was a fatal mistake they made in their life. If they had ignored me, slighted me and made me feel no warmth but hatred for family, they would have saved me. They were so kind and understanding, and always looked at you with so much affection that you would feel uncomfortable. We were quite wealthy then, which I did not know until later. My father used to be a bank clerk. He was always quiet at home, as if he had never existed. Both these gave rise to what happened later. When those aiming to confiscate our property came in, my father was listening to the radio on the sofa in the living room. According to my mother, it seemed that he never planned to stop those big men. He barely stood up, and did nothing but keep calling my mother's nickname. I heard my mother begging those men to wait outside the bathroom and telling them that her daughter was having a bath. It was something to that effect. She kept on begging.

"They came in, nearly twenty men, all muscular. They did

not even look at me, as if they were uninterested in a naked teenage girl. They struck the bathtub madly with gymnastic sticks and iron rods. They knew beforehand that my father had hid his gold bar in the bathtub. They did not let me go. They did not look at me or smile dirtily. They just kept striking the bathtub, panting. The water flowed past the corridor to the living room, to my father's feet. It was unbelievable that he was still sitting there. The radio was still on, broadcasting women's chorus of something like 'Red Guards coming to Tiananmen.'

"My mother became crazy. She tried desperately to stop them, and they broke her left leg. They smashed the bathtub and found what they came for, a gold bar. The rest of all were in the chest of drawers in the bedroom. That was apparently my father's foible, not a motive for hiding.

"Those men ignored me. And it was their pretended neglect that made me see myself clearly as a woman. I cannot remember the face of any one of them, but I remember every movement. In that very month, my period came early. Since then, I had been longing for a man until I was married. But I have never reached orgasm. I want to see men, but I enjoy no sexual pleasure. I want to die every time I have sex. That's all." Her narration came to a stop, and she waited for Luo Ke's response. But there was none.

17

Aunt Tao Bo'er was a rare faithful reader of bizarre stories. She led her ordinary but substantial life with the company of a series of detective stories. Conan Doyle, Agatha Christie and Simenon are three main sources of her world view that cannot be induced. Aunt Tao Bo'er thought that detectives, especially private detectives, were the most trustworthy gentlemen on earth, and that their thinking, as well as their lives, was in good order, in sharp contrast to the chaotic world. She even disseminated a dystopian remark in private that the world should be ruled by those smart detectives. Aunt Tao Bo'er's knowledge was not enough to allow her to write a thesis on this aspect, otherwise it would create many problems for the dignified academia. Anytime within a day, Aunt Tao Bo'er would tell you all about the heroic deeds of Sherlock Holmes, Poirot and Maigret as long as she was in the mood for it. At the same time, she would put on a frightened and confused look to scare you. But people always thought it was a trick of Aunt Tao Bo'er to amuse them, without feeling her fear inside. Ultimately, Aunt Tao Bo'er was always terrified by her own retelling and came back to her small room with a grim face to continue knitting. One day, she met a real detective in her life. It was an amiable middle-aged man, who dressed well and smelled fragrant, like a fashionable woman who put on too much face cream. Vigorous muscle at the crook of his arm bulged in his suit with slim sleeves, which evoked the picture of him shoveling coal in front of a steaming boiler. When the detective came in, Aunt Tao Bo'er was lying on her side by the window, bathing in the ray of sunlight reflected by the glass and groaning. "Hello. I'm here to make some inquiries. This is my license." The detective presented a small black booklet under Aunt Tao Bo'er's nose. "Ah, smells nice." During that time she was very sick, and she looked at the stranger in front of her with hazy eyes. "Who are you?" "I'm here to make friends with you." "Friends? I don't need friends." Aunt Tao Bo'er started blabbering, "I only make friends with my family members. My grandmother told me that everything should start within a family. Outsiders are dangerous." The "detective" came for Luo Ke but had to go back as he encountered such a sick old lady who should speak in such a natural manner.

Aunt Tao Bo'er was among those who were called spinsters by neighbors. At the same time, she was good at feigning ignorance, which people did not know. Thirty years ago, on a summer evening with a cool breeze, seated in Carlton Theatre, a young man she had just met was uttering sweet words and reaching out his right hand to her breast. Aunt Tao Bo'er was then a decent woman. Furious as she was, she pretended to be composed and asked in a loud voice, "What are you doing?"

In Luo Ke's eyes, Aunt Tao Bo'er was a lonely but lovely old woman. She had no hobbies or collections except the detective storybooks with yellowed covers and the sweater she kept knitting and taking apart and reknitting. Luo Ke once asked her why she did not marry. "Marriage is laughable," Aunt Tao Bo'er guffawed, "but of course, remaining single is as much laughable."

On the evening after the detective's visit, Aunt Tao Bo'er seemed to be startled by the actualization of her lifelong interest and was sent to hospital before dinner. She died of heart attack that night. Before she passed away, she cryptically muttered to Luo Ke, "That was a police officer." They were Aunt Tao Bo'er's last words.

Luo Ke had always been missing her. She was a good person, who never disturbed others with her own foibles and followed her heart without falling into stubbornness. Her unusual sanguinity brought him many comfortable and happy episodes.

The detective—according to Aunt Tao Bo'er's last words, the police officer—did not appear again. No one knew what happened that afternoon. Luo Ke's father blamed Luo Ke for her death, as the mystery man had only come because of him, but Luo Ke tried hard to defend that it was probably just Aunt Tao Bo'er's hallucination. It remained unsolved, the answer to which Aunt Tao Bo'er had taken away. Meanwhile, it also became the excuse of Luo Yizhi to lash out at his son. Partly to avoid his father's rebuke and partly to follow his heart, Luo Ke moved out temporarily.

18

Less than half a year after the Communist Youth League Apartment Building was completed, a large piece of cement ground outside the building was turned into a parking lot that charged fees. Another half year passed and the ground once as smooth as a runway was covered with cinder. The first time Luo Ke and Yin Mang came to the apartment building with a box of books and a thermos bottle, a Toyota Crown luxury sedan and a cargo truck with a No. 49XXX license plate were competing to enter the parking lot. The dust storm they threw up, combined with the black smoke from the non-local truck with a diesel engine, made the entrance of the apartment building look like the exterior of a gangster movie—things blown up and down. Yin Mang came up with a nickname for the parking lot—"Rolling Stones Avenue." To commemorate the beginning of their couple life, which was a little conspicuous, she came up with a private countersign for the apartment—"Mick Jagger Apartment." But the wordplay, which was more or less boring, was soon forgotten, like the gatekeeper and the once extremely irritating lift attendant. The two fellows, similar in age yet different in character, were completely qualified as typecast actors in shoddy movies. "Just ignore them," Yin Mang said. "And what you can only do is to ignore them," concluded Luo Ke.

The room was rented. The landlady was a celibate woman, who was sent to a mental hospital right after renovating the house. Neighbors said that she was a flirty woman with many ex-boyfriends. As for the details, Luo Ke and Yin Mang were unable to know.

Having learned lessons from the mental patient He Dafen, they made huge noises from time to time, laughing (from Aunt Tao Bo'er), screaming a part of the instruction book of the washing machine, turning up the player to a deafening volume, and banging the door when they went out. It was less than a week before the neighbors saw them as a mad couple and became worried about their assumed lifelong marriage. The one who suffered the greatest loss was He Dafen. The gentlewoman who had to rent the apartment was now in a white strait jacket. Every time the door to the corridor with a spring lock had to be opened with great strength, and the kitchen sink was often clogged by cigarette butts, fish bones, bread crumbs, tea leaves, tangled hair and sometimes even a broken pencil. Luo Ke and Yin Mang had to roll up their sleeves and take care of the greasy sink. Fallen sparks of cigarettes had burned tiny holes in the dark green acrylic carpet, on which there were also coffee and wine stains caused by accidental spills. They had taken the liberty of replacing for many times the stylus of the hi-fi record player with an inferior stylus. There was nothing wrong with the stylus, but Luo Ke somehow caused it to make a harsh noise on the delicate record every time it rewound automatically. The honorable list of the injured included two big names, the Beatles and Bruce Springsteen. One day at noon, however, Yin Mang put Puccini's *Turandot* on the player. After a few rounds when the chorus had just sang "In Turandot's homeland executioners were always busy" in the prelude, the damned stylus made a deep scratch on the bright surface of the record. Then they stopped using the player forever.

19

During the times when Luo Ke and Yin Mang were deep in love, there were fewer and fewer clear days in the south. Those who fiddled with glass test tubes and accurate charts all day long used those so-called "scientific" terms to describe the horrible dust and blackish clouds which would eventually produce acid rain in the sky above the city.

The grey cloud sheets that blocked the sun hung over the people walking in a hurry or standing at loss on the streets. As to the elderly and the young wandering on the banks of the muddy river, they were constantly breathing its stinky volatiles. By the winding river which had bred as many southern talents as idiots, the city landscape was changing in a slow and cautious manner. People met and parted, experiencing the sorrow and fantastic lure of life's capriciousness. They became numb alcoholics with sighs and groans, and all ended up by a small window of a small room in a hospital. Or, driven by a stupid kind of enthusiasm, they went to a public place or some nook to behave in an extremely bewildering fashion, and ended up in a heavily guarded clinic as a mental patient.

It was the eccentric liking and the excessively stubborn faith that made the lovesick He Dafen a model of taking medicine on time. Every time the solemn-looking female care worker gave out pills, her pale face would beam with joy. "Oh, look how much she loves those pills!" the nurses said to each other, amazed. Days flew away with those complimentary remarks, while He Dafen's face noticeably bloated. With varicose veins and sagging muscles, her hair, like leaves in an autumn wind, took away her peaceful look. Though the unmarried woman was rendered muddle-headed by the medicine, her cloudy eyes would still radiate joyful brilliance once a nurse flashed a bottle of pills in front of her. At that time, her comrades, the other mental patients, would gather to watch her happy and intoxicated look. Her neighbor, a lanky woman with a quick mind and outstanding eloquence, said abruptly to a nurse, "It is irredeemable that comrade He Dafen should enjoy taking medicine so much." "Yes," He Dafen said, "and there is no medicine that I haven't taken. Is there any medicine that I haven't taken in the world?" She questioned the nurse. The ill-willed nurse had intended to say no, but she actually said, "There were a lot of kinds of medicine that you haven't taken in the world." The syntax perfectly matched the language of He Dafen, and the female medicine addict was very much satisfied.

There were still some pleasant sunny days that made people unable to sit still. On such a day Luo Ke and Yin Mang went to the suburbs to visit their landlady. It was a prerequisite for renting the house. This humane and boring visit remained a vivid memory. In the coach madly roaring forward, Luo Ke and Yin Mang kept being bounced by the seats wrapped with cracked faux leather for over an hour and finally got off at the stop near a concrete bridge. Under the bridge some waterfowls were gliding leisurely near a rusty boat, as if completely unaware of their unpredictable life in the future. It was a peaceful pastoral scene aloof from the rest of the world. Luo Ke and Yin Mang, faces covered by dust and mouths filled with sand, trotted along the way after parting from the ducks and swans. They caught up with a man, who was striding forward with arms swinging. With a few exchanges, they learned that he was going the same place and then decided to go there with the company of this vigorous man. "Right there. About fifteen minutes." The handsome man said in a voice that revealed his enthusiasm, casually pointing at something in the distance with his long index finger.

He led the way ahead, with arms swinging back and forth as if paddling. The sun at noon shone directly on the asphalt road, creating a warm atmosphere. Nothing could make one drowsier than being led by a stranger to a hospital one had never visited. The situation was of typical significance to Luo Ke. In his dreamy memory, he always played the role of a follower. He followed his mother on the bank where waves lapped; he followed the teacher playing leapfrog, whose face he could not remember, on the football pitch where the pupils were throwing up sand and dust; he followed his peers who had wide knowledge and good memory, reciting such famous quotes with them anytime anywhere as "the core power that leads our cause" and "you young people are in the prime of life, full of vitality"; he also followed the carriages of a nearby riding stable on the way home after school. On a lucky day when the young driving soldier was not that stubborn, he would clumsily climb onto the carriage and ride for fifty to a hundred meters and then jump off and head home.

"You two are going there to check in, right?" the man leading the way asked amiably. "No, we are going to visit a patient." "Visit a patient … Well, then where does he or she live?" "In Unit No.4." "That model unit," the man said with a longing look. "Are you also going there to visit someone?" Yin Mang asked. "No, I'm from the hospital," he said in a tone that made it seem like he were saying "Hospital is my home."

Walking on the suburban road, the three started talking. But the conversation became a monologue of the man "from the hospital" after they had walked out a hundred meters. "You two seem well-educated. To tell you the truth, I can figure out an intellectual the moment I see him. Ah, do you have any hobbies?" the man "from the hospital" suddenly asked cryptically. "What hobbies?" Luo Ke and Yin Mang asked immediately. "What hobbies? What else? Yueju opera!" he giggled. "Intellectuals like Yueju opera! Intellectuals are Yueju opera! ..." Most of the things one came across by accident could make one frightened. Yin Mang was so nauseated that she wanted to give him a couple of slaps. They were certain that the womanish guide who equated Yueju opera with intellectuals was a mental patient. At the moment they were heading to the hospital to visit He Dafen with his company. Who in the world could ask a fellow with mental disorder to pay attention to others' reaction? Though Luo Ke and Yin Mang were gnashing their teeth, the man "from the hospital" was still battering, "Yueju opera is exquisite. Yueju opera is noble. Yueju opera is good at displaying love between man and woman. Love is noble. Love is exquisite. The consummate embodiment of love is in Yueju opera. In art, Yueju opera is ..."

20

After receiving the trunk call from Sidney, Luo Ke stayed at home for a whole week instead of going to the shop on work, without any excuse. The shop manager once called to confirm if he was ill. "Yes, I'm seriously ill," Luo Ke grumbled angrily on the phone. He felt that he was lashing out at a giant object, to which all people belonged.

No sooner had the shop manager's cheerful and encouraging voice been gone than the mellow voice of Zhu Ke, an old friend of Luo Ke, started bubbling on the phone after a few rings.

"Luo Ke, how are you?" Zhu Ke, as always, feigned cordiality with an exaggerated tone.

"It's a year since you last called me. How are you?"

"I'm so busy. Now I'm studying *The Book of Changes*! You know, I have broad interests ..."

Luo Ke thought that there were indeed quite a few people in this world with broad interests and full energy. There must be a lot of vitamin pills and protein shots under their pillow. Zhu Ke was an epitome in this respect. He played with harmonica, *erhu*, dulcimer, *pipa*, moon zither, accordion, organ, violin, guitar, electronic organ and piano, and had a not bad command of all of these instruments. His diversions included cricket fighting, mahjong, poker, go, chess, Chinese checkers, army chess, and naval chess. He had written short stories, novellas and trilogies. In terms of poetry, his works included short poems, suite poems, long poems, blank verses and even metrical poems, and the word "epic" was marked on the flyleaf of a booklet with a red cover. He had also written some plays and TV and movie scripts. The most remarkable accomplishment of Zhu Ke, the versatile man, was one of his works named *New Philosophy*, in which he was said to establish the Chinese philosophical school. He once disseminated the message that he planned to make a copy of the manuscript and send it to UNESCO. Luo Ke had read the outline of this monumental work, which recounted his copious personal experience in 200,000 words. He thought it was probably more appropriate to call it Zhu Ke's memoir (Or intellectual history?).

"Zhu Ke, I remember that you have already studied *The Book of Changes*."

"There is always something new in reading and rereading. And this time I incorporate *qigong* in my study."

"I guess so." It was the trend of that time. Luo Ke had always admired Zhu Ke's inexhaustible creativity. What those Tolstoys had devoted their life to only took those young men like Zhu Ke one month to finish in the twentieth century. And they still had time to show up on all occasions, to engage extensively in social activities, and to display their eloquence among different groups of people. Luo Ke thought on Zhu Ke's behalf that living a life like this was indeed respectable and comfortable.

"Hey, Luo Ke. Don't you feel anything? I'm transmitting my power to you now on the phone."

"Don't give me an electric shock. If you have anything to tell me, just say it."

"You'll never guess who I met. Yin Mang. You know what happened? She was divorced."

"Have you gone mad because of *qigong*? You must have bumped into a ghost."

"Don't give me that *Strange-Stories-from-a-Chinese-Studio* crap, or stuff like the human-ghost relationship. A living woman, seriously."

"I received a call from Sun Shu a week ago. He said she was dead."

"Don't you get it? He was trying to make you sick." This, Luo Ke could comprehend. Zhu Ke was among those who were used to defining human beings as people who disgusted each other. His personal hatred for others might surpass a racial counterpart. He was always actively involved in all kinds of disputes, acting as a witness, an investigator, an accessory, a spokesman, a clerk, or a moral arbitrator. He helped others to make plans and to look into the future regularly. Normally, he always managed to mix his personal delusion with the public opinion. He disseminated every message with a noble principle attached, as if he was reciting the Bible.

"Hey, Luo Ke. Aren't you going to see her? She has come all the way across the ocean." Luo Ke could almost see Zhu Ke wagging his steaming head in the dirty collar. "You know what, Luo Ke went to see Yin Mang."

"You go see her. She likes you," said Luo Ke.

It was as unfair to say that Yin Mang liked Zhu Ke as it was to say that Zhu Ke liked Yin Mang. They were like a pair of natural enemies, crossing verbal swords once they met. Over time, they almost became partners. Even if they ran into each other on the street, they must stop under a telegraph pole and start a round. The most well-known example took place in a summer. Zhu Ke and Yin Mang met with each other at the corner of Medical School Road, which became a classic encounter battle. Both were tongue-tied because of lack of preparation. Almost at the same time, however, they saw the advertisement for exchanging houses on the telegraph pole by the road. Their topic that day was "the sociological significance and success rate" of putting up advertisements for exchanging houses on the street. One side of the debate was a silly young man, the other a silly young girl.

21

Of course, it was amusing to recall the historic moment when they met for the first time. If wild imagination and unrestrained fiction could satisfy the creative impulse of normal people, then the faithful imitation of something would undoubtedly occupy a higher position. The carefully arranged party was absolutely worth reproducing even with unskillful writing, as it gathered outstanding talents together, including experienced and brave soldiers like Zhu Ke and Yin Mang.

Ms. Jian Ying, the hostess, was a benevolent middle-aged woman keen on art. But her unusual beauty and attractive look—with black tight clothes when greeting a houseful of guests—made her seem extraordinarily young. All the artists and would-be artists of different generations unanimously acclaimed her as an extremely rare art patron in southern China. During the party, Ms. Jian Ying smilingly greeted everybody present in high spirits. The guests kept smoking, drinking, and stuffing their mouths with dessert, from which little crumbs fell, and littered peels all around. Soon, the air in the house reminded one of the big pool in a communal bathhouse. Nevertheless, Ms. Jian Ying, still amiable, offered cigarettes and tea from time to time or just sat up right and listened attentively, like an Asian Madame von Meck or even Madame de Warens. Inspired by the hospitality of the hostess, some great expressions, obscure theories, vulgar jokes and boring news started coming up one after another. Everyone was a speaker, and no one paid attention to what others were saying. Ms. Jian Ying was the only real listener. She benignly watched the huddle of old kids and little adults making a racket with an understanding smile on her face, fancy words like structure, existence, perception and transcendence flying to and fro under the whitewashed ceiling. In the meanwhile, Zhu Ke and Yin Mang had argued for a long time about the comparison between O. Henry the story king and Barthelme the story retailer. During their argument, Luo Ke savored all the edible things without a break and introduced to a well-acquainted young poet some delicious dessert like the mille-feuille, the log cake, and the whipped cream. Any dessert connected with cream would delight him. He listened for a while on Yin Mang's side, yet still failed to understand what they were talking about. Therefore he whispered in her ear, recommending her to try the desirable dessert and then retreated to a room to watch TV.

"Are you feeling unwell, young man?" Ms. Jian Ying sat down, her attractive body close to Luo Ke. A group of female dancers with few clothes on were jumping madly on TV.

"No, I'm just a couch potato." Luo Ke glanced at Yin Mang, who was craning her neck and making gestures toward Zhu Ke, and then turned back. "Do you know all these people here?"

"Almost."

"You must have had enough. They all eat a lot."

"You know them well."

"Not much. If you listen to them talking about Huntington or Toffler, it's as if they were exactly these two Americans. You can never figure out who they are." In this tongue twister pattern, they chatted in front of the television for quite a while. The party came to a pause when Zhu Ke accidentally broke a glass. He ran to Luo Ke and said in a hoarse voice, "I was defeated. The woman who came with you was really eloquent. I'm so embarrassed that I must leave now." Then he left in a hurry.

Later Yin Mang told Luo Ke that Zhu Ke was not really discussing problems with her. He was only obsessed with his own voice and wanted to hear it while talking, and therefore he lost immediately when his voice grew hoarse.

Parties at Ms. Jian Ying's house were like a small station on a wilderness of art. Few of its visitors were interested in going back. What was more, the sexy woman in black was apparently more or less mysterious. Several years after that night, there were rumors about Ms. Jian Ying. Different versions gave others the impression that she ran a gangster inn like Sun Erniang, who specialized in making steamed buns stuffed with human flesh. According to one version, she was jailed in Qinghai Province because she resold antiques. Some said that since she spent too much yet could hardly make ends meet, she had no choice but to take up prostitution. In retrospect, it was those eloquent hangers-on that had played on her.

Every time Luo Ke thought of those ridiculous scenes, he felt sorry for her. Such a decent woman was wasted by art, which was worth nothing. His tender thought did not come out of nowhere. It was not because people's tongues became her grave, but because her house made Luo Ke associate with some odd things in the past that Aunt Tao Bo'er had talked about. One place in Tao Bo'er's narration was none other than the Dehong Villa in which Ms. Jian Ying and more than a dozen neighbors lived together. Its first hostess was the fifth wife of a Chinese Malaysian captain. Among the numerous lovers of this flirty woman named Yu'er who came from a brothel was Tao Lie, Luo Ke's cousin. The story was so complicated that it had never been clearly narrated by the paranoid Aunt Tao Bo'er. She always inferred that her bad memory made her suffer so much in that she could not even remember the face of her adopted son. Nevertheless, as a faithful reader of detective stories, Aunt Tao Bo'er, like an experienced detective, properly recollected some details and physical evidence, including the names Yu'er and Dehong Villa. She placed a particular emphasis on a carved screen made of rosewood. "He ran everywhere day and night like a mad man with that thing on his shoulder." He died of gonorrhea in the end.

22

Some things could not be recalled from the beginning to the end. No one could figure out their edges and infiltrate into the delicate inside. It was like a boy splitting a length of an oak tree chopped down with an axe. In the meanwhile he knew nothing about it and only came to know the secret in an extremely blind state. Luo Ke appeared to have found himself looking back into the past in his old age, but he still remained at a loss for what he did. He realized in a trance that he was walking in a dream, wearily floating on his feet. The air around him seemed to have been dyed blue, with an inviting scent that the nose could not detect. It misled one into thinking that every moment he experienced now was a fragment of his previous life covered with dust and relief portrait hidden under despair, which evoked reminiscent feelings in one's heart. In the evening, when the street quieted down a little, Luo Ke inserted his index finger in the Perspex rotary dial before the endless stillness of the night came. Suddenly, the familiar group of numbers poured into his memory in an extremely unfamiliar way, like a greeting in the distance, though it did not seem to have been invited. It just hung around him, like an ancient tune caught by the unprepared ear. If he did not plan to make a phone call with death, then he must want to pass the unconfirmed death without effort. Luo Ke's anxiety, however, made him more fidgety than being away from Yin Mang in the end. He had imagined that a certain scene having repeated innumerable times in the past days would reappear in an unexpected way. When the impossible voice came back to life and back to Luo Ke's life again, it made him more confused than when it was first reflected on the screen of his heart. He tried many times but could not get the call through. As if under the anticipation before orgasm for the body's future state, he suddenly felt he had walked to the extremity of a known area. He could no longer deceive himself and thought that there had always been the expectation for endless possible returns hiding deep in his heart. He was no longer able to indulge his unbridled imagination again and again. He must change his way, and let concrete things wake himself up instead of stubbornly viewing life as a reservoir, where people dived without fear of storm or undercurrent and made all kinds of moves only to match the ripples caused by their stroking. Luo Ke thought to himself that it was absurd to make such daily metaphors guided by his thinking, as he could address his tangled personal experience in an abstract way and avoid some completely unnecessary connection between the rudder of pain and the turbulence of environment. He felt that he was willing to bow his head towards worldly possessions and submit to the abandonment and the eradication of personal sentiment.

Luo Ke reflected that he kept travelling and lingering in places casually chosen at inappropriate times, and such a situation with double unluckiness gave him a sense of consciousness. He only discovered his image from the inside, but he could never scrutinize the outside look of his image. It was arranged out of his sight by fate, hidden in broad daylight like an invisible order, and its apparent complexity rendered every external exploration vain. He did not touch the milky white body of the telephone again, and kept away from it, as if letting his body fall into the empty oblivion. Just like this, he sat in the room quietly, thoughts wandering, incapable of touching the meaning or the boundary of anything. Luo Ke could not choose between Yin Mang and Xiang An. He always managed to detect the astonishing similarity between one woman and another in an instant but neglected their subtle differences. He never discriminated between them and therefore never felt the novelty of each one of them as an individual. Their tenderness, meticulous observation of others' mind, and care and opportune neglect of others' sensitivity. Their deep affection when embracing a man, worship of faith when refusing others with a smile, and their addiction to stunning beauty and gaudy appearance. They excelled in pointing out men's embarrassing mistakes but lost no time expressing their leniency. As to sex, their conventional attitude never prevented them from being carried away when they indulged in passion, which was even harder for Luo Ke to tell the difference. In a deep sorrow, he looked at the typical dark sky in the south outside the window and let dreams and memories fleet in mind. He could touch neither the ending of the incident nor the distant beginning annihilated by time. At this moment, the elusive memories became a block between hearts, which was a symbol and a real object at the same time, blocking everything. Luo Ke and his lover looked at each other on the two sides of the screen of time, lost in thought. He inadvertently recalled his cousin he had never met, the man running on the southern streets in 1949, dragging a screen. He did not manage to run away from the ending brought by his romantic experiences. His ridiculous life had given him grave despair and great compassion. As the blind man of Buenos Aires said, "Fate can be merciless with the slightest distraction."

Luo Ke could not see all of this as some abstract or oneiric revelation. He dimly felt that the words he exchanged with his lover in the past also became a phenomenal screen on such a night. Every new meeting meant carrying the screen along one more time. At last the vibration of the air led to the collapse of specific emotions, which made intervals nothingness, and looking out into the distance a pure posture.

Volume II

1

When Luo Ke woke up, he felt his face glowing. Last night before going to bed, he soaked his feet in hot water and spent quite a while brushing his teeth carefully. Then he went to bed with a mouthful of the scent of the White Jade toothpaste. As he slept well, Luo Ke thought he looked better in the mirror than in reality. The freckles on his face (some said it was a sign of sexual desire and others said it foreboded cancer) seemed less noticeable after the soap was applied, which gave him more anxiety and less joy. Luo Ke was oversensitive to health. A headache, a sneeze and a running nose could all make him fidgety and remind him of the desperate fight between leucocytes and viruses. No matter which part of his body was funny, the first thing he did was picking up the home health handbook and looking it up. When he found its medical term and related instructions, he would rummage through the closet for the needed medicine and then took it with water. Only till then did he finish his job. Luo Ke believed in moderation, which he explained as smoking moderately, working moderately and talking moderately (some said it was most exhausting to talk with others)—namely, no self-indulgence.

At ten in the morning, Luo Ke took out from the mailbox downstairs a letter with a blue and white envelope from Fälön. Back to his room, he picked up the scissor on the desk and gave it a cut. A smooth white piece of paper fell into his hand. It was a letter from an old friend called Xu Bing, his deskmate in the middle school who had slept in class with him. Luo Ke identified him from the neat pen writing on the letter. Outside the window, the sun was shining brightly. Several sparrows were taking a walk in the yard in a seemingly leisurely manner but vigilantly hopped from time to time, which revealed their frightened heart. It was quiet all around, a good time for reading a letter from far away. Luo Ke had not contacted Xu Bing during the last five or six years. He vaguely recalled that in the previous letter Xu Bing told him that he was taken in by a glib conman on the street. He bought four brown Dutch rabbits (God knows what they are) from a cardboard box on his bicycle. Before he kept them at home for a week, they invited a group of mice. The four four-legged animals named brown Dutch rabbits by the glib middle-aged man joined the mice that intruded into his house without any hesitation. The flock was busy climbing into the rice barrel, gnawing table legs and squeaking. "They cost me ten yuan (approximately 2 US dollars)," he grumbled miserably in the letter.

Xu Bing was a shy young man and had a handsome face with big eyes and a high nose bridge. Sometimes he gave others an overly gentle impression. He put the word "dear" in front of Luo Ke's name, which startled him to some extent. Then he said he was cheated again (Who would believe him?), but this time in Sweden, a freezing country. After graduation from the middle school, Xu Bing was sent to the Southern Ocean Corporation and became a little seaman who painted the sail (according to himself). He had been to harbors of many different countries in these years, which, in his words, was "travelling around." This time he was cheated by a prostitute at the harbor of Fälön. Oh, that cheater was so skilled that she let him helplessly watch the "Flying Pigeon" sail away. Now he could only (Only?) stay in Sweden. "I am so easily taken in." Luo Ke almost saw him talking with a prostitute on the Simmons mattress in his bedroom in Fälön about his yearning for home in a foreign country. After describing the customs of the tranquil Scandinavian country as an evasion, he wrote, "To be honest, girls in Fälön are quite open." He specially pointed out that he was not talking about prostitutes. "I'm afraid of catching STD, so I haven't done that, not even once. I still live alone." Luo Ke heaved a sigh, rubbed his eyes and examined the stamp and postmark on the envelope. Fälön, Sweden. No problem. Luo Ke pondered over the meaning of this unexpected letter. Did Xu Bing send it just to report to his old classmate and friend that he was still keeping his virginity in an "open" place? Luo Ke read the ambiguous letter twice and eventually threw it in the drawer. "He was always conned on the street," he concluded. Luo Ke immediately wrote a letter in reply. First he seriously criticized his classmate for betraying their country, and wrote, "Since your ship has gone, there is no choice but to stay there. Since you are now conned into a high welfare society, you'd better be wary of being conned into some third world country, like Vietnam." Xu Bing had mentioned in the letter that there were many Vietnamese in Fälön. "I have been to Vietnam," Luo Ke continued to write. "There was nothing other than incessant rains and cartridges everywhere." Luo Ke laughed to himself, "I almost stayed there."

Luo Ke folded the letter several times into a crossed Z shape, the two sides covering each other. If the person who received the letter was careless and opened the letter without thinking, it would be torn in half and he could only read it with one piece in each hand. This was a trick that Luo Ke played on letter collectors. He put the folded letter in an envelope, took a pen, and mechanically copied the two addresses on Xu Bing's envelope, swapping the left and right part. Then he stuck a stamp on it and sealed the opening, and trotted to the newly painted old mailbox on the nearby street. The moment he pushed the letter in with one hand, he suddenly woke up. As if dreaming in messiness, he could not remember the face value of the stamp he stuck on the letter that was going to travel across the ocean, and had no choice but to wait for its return.

He walked back in frustration, his mood suddenly turning

bad. No sooner had he stepped into the corridor than he heard a shriek of an electric drill competing with a brick wall. And what followed was a scream of a mini grinder cutting wood from the dentist Zhang Rongtian's house. The eldest son of the dentist started the huge project to renovate the house for marriage.

"Right," Luo Ke thought, "happiness and unhappiness all start with clamor."

Sixty years ago, Aunt Tao Bo'er and Tao Lie, Luo Ke's young cousin, went to the lively city on the eastern coastline on a chugging steam train from the north. They set foot on a wet southern street in an afternoon after a September rain. Even then, Tao Lie cherished his faith as much as Aunt Tao Bo'er cherished her fear created by the combination of books and imagination. Tao Lie, who walked with a wobble, valued sensory pleasure. The fragrance of powder from young women, white gardenias placed on a wet handkerchief on a street stand, the composing and delicate mixed scent of plants vaguely wafting from a tea store, and even the special smell in a tobacco shop were all unforgettable to him. Tao Lie soon took to the city with different kinds of people. The heterogeneous life consisting of the streetscape and those wandering residents woke up Tao Lie's roving instinct in an instant. Soon he quit from a private school and hung around in theatres and rich ladies' living rooms, sending away many days with flirting and boring nonsense.

The rumors and speculations about Tao Lie made Luo Ke dream of the showy and astonishing scenes of his cousin's activities many times: On a coolest summer day, a breeze swept away humidity. At the corner of a lonely alley filled with the refreshing air after rain, Tao Lie, in white poplin clothes, sat cross-legged on a pedicab with a sandalwood folding fan in hand. On his side was his furniture—the tri-fold carved rosewood screen, his "Yu'er."

The screen was given to him by a concubine of the Malaysian captain of a merchant ship. The woman from northern Suzhou living in a Spanish-style house was named "Yu'er." Yu'er moved into Dehong Villa from Fourth Avenue overnight, and at the same speed, she hooked up and slept with Tao Lie, the playboy sitting next to her in theatre when they were watching the Peking opera *Splitting the Coffin Open*. The erotic performance evoked her memories in the brothel and the trying time in an empty house as a concubine wetted the front seats of the Queen Theatre. Before the opera ended, Yu'er held Tao Lie's fair-skinned hand and fled from the theatre.

On that beautiful night, Yu'er and Tao Lie caressed each other on the captain's bed. Yu'er was a provocative woman with wild imagination in sex, though the blurry scene of her gracefully taking off her clothes behind the screen was more intoxicating to Tao Lie. It was like the introduction played by the flute in an overture, which foreboded everything and woke up everything. On the flyleaf of Tao Lie's personal history, Yu'er conveniently signed her name. Her influence on him was incredible. Their relationship ended when the Malaysian captain sailed back. Yu'er gave the screen to Tao Lie when they bid farewell in tears, but it did not occur to her that what she gave to the young man was more than a screen carved with a pair of phoenixes. In Tao Lie's dissipated life afterwards, he developed an obsession related with sex. If he did not bring his "Yu'er" and unfold it in front of the bed, he could only weep in the corner. Therefore, he hired a pedicab and visited every brothel with his screen. But in less than half a year, the debauched life drew to an end as the screen was lost. Tao Lie became an alcoholic and was drunk all day in the life of chasing women. He could never figure out in front of whose bed he left his "Yu'er." Tao Lie, with only skin and bones, mourned for his loss and fell sick, raving day and night. After nine days, the playboy who indulged in carnal pleasure developed ulcers all over his body. With another nine days passing by, he died while mumbling "Yu'er." The stench in the room lingered for a long time in the house of the Luos.

Now it was already a few years since Aunt Tao Bo'er passed away, but the admonitory significance of Tao Lie's ups and downs was enduring. It must be pointed out that Luo Ke was a careless man. Even though he could recite fifty ways of keeping good health, he would only manage to follow three to five of them at best, which still depended on whether he lost his mind in relationships. Luo Ke walked around the kitchen restlessly and smelled here and there, hunting for breakfast. At last, he poured himself a large glass of cool boiled water, took out a half piece of bread from the fridge, put himself on a chair and started eating in a leisurely manner. He was used to this kind of breakfast. Sometimes he would add a fried egg or a glass of milk, depending on whether he felt like it. Anything more extravagant, like a glass of orange juice, would be less likely, of course, unless someone gave him a treat. On the writing desk or the couch with a crimson cover, or in the kitchen cupboard, some delicious things would suddenly turn up, such as a boxful of canned beer, an carton of imported cigarettes, a small box of dessert from Ruby Foods, a basket of local specialties and so on, all from his father's friends and their friends. If Luo Ke happened to be in the mood, he would finish them in a blink.

The skilled craftsmen downstairs put aside the electric tools in their hands, but almost at the same time, saws began singing merrily. Luo Ke thought he would rather go out for a walk than sit alone at home in distress.

2

Sometimes Luo Ke would imagine himself living in another century. The twenty-first century, for example, was not a dream too wild. As long as you did not encounter those thugs or unfortunate incidents in the movies, you should never be involved with the stiff doctors devoted to science too frequently. They would intimidate you with those strange and difficult terms, making you feel ashamed in front of those people with glowing faces and great strength and bitterly sympathetic with those with the same disease. Hiding among common people, you could happily live for up to a century. On other days when Luo Ke was lost in his reverie, he wished to live in the nineteenth century, which, according to artists' enthusiastic discussion, was full of romantic masters. He even thought for sure that what flew in the blood vessels of romanticists was not blood, but fragrant wine. Unless one was obsessed with accurate facts, he would always spend one or two days in his life roaming in the sweet paradise of imagination.

Luo Ke often privately met those characters in classics, regardless of details such as time, the location, the language or the interest. Most importantly, he did not consider its feasibility. No one had discovered even one of such absurd things that would otherwise easily incur criticism, as it was easy to meet a guy who liked daydreaming but the chance to catch him daydreaming was slim. Nevertheless, there were still things in the world that fulfilled people's wishes after all. If two people who liked daydreaming met each other, then something good would naturally come out of it.

No two individuals were more alike than Luo Ke and Yin Mang in terms of indulgence in fantasy, talent for gluttony and sloth, obsession with some quiet southern streets, the lazy look, and poor frowning faces. Apart from those, what best demonstrated the similarity of this engaged couple was their anticipation and preparation for giving up a lifelong relationship in spite of the fact that they were in love. And they did not plan to hide the intention from each other. Every time they made love, they could discover its trace, sound and hypnotic enchantment. When they listened to the music on the radio on a night of full moon, the delicate emotional ripples ignited by the rhythm out of their mind's control, as regular as sounds made by a metronome, aroused desolation like the silver chips beyond words in the shadow of swaying branches. They listened to the doubt of the world with doubt, as if it would loom from where it did not exist and knock on the heart of the despairing waiter who had already stopped waiting for a long time.

Bathed in such a winding sentimental current, he did not experience anything close to the deception involved in a relationship. Six days ago, when an unexpected phone call induced Luo Ke's rippling wild thoughts, Xiang An had performed in the prelude of another wedding drama. Luo Ke still could not find any sign that his slow mind failed to perceive. On which debauched night, or at which debauched moment, did Xiang An fall in love with this Chinese American guy? They were barely of the same height even if he wore a pair of shiny leather shoes with soles as thick as a horse's hooves while she stood in bare feet. Luo Ke firmly believed that she did have the talent to shuffle between two theatres, and that she could devote herself to portraying characters of the same kind in the two dramas—a pure, innocent lover. She was willing to accept success achieved from either of them. It was hard to know since when there were some secret coquetry only for men to identify in her refined behavior and the tempting charm impossible to hide was shining in her unconscious glance, appealing to the opposite sex.

While Luo Ke was rowing hard on the boat of the past, Richard Ma, owner of the Tang Dynasty Restaurant, was touring the green mountains and clear rivers in Hangzhou, Zhejiang Province—the paradise on earth—arm in arm with Xiang An.

Mr. Ma's restaurant was not like a grand ancient state as its name suggested. It was sandwiched between a supermarket and a small movie theatre with seventy seats. The apricot flag embroidered with its name was like an ancient banner for conjuring spirits, repeatedly waving on one side of the Stars and Stripes toward Xiang An, who lived through a bumpy journey with good acting skills. Mr. Ma, an adorable, dark-skinned man of small but strong build in his forties, was good at imitating the big American kids' manner. He managed to call himself Xiang An's third father (husband father) in front of her biological father (who she committed incest with) and her (naive) foster father. Nothing was difficult since there were three fathers taking care of one daughter.

Before Xiang An was finally taken abroad by their late marriage, the couple, both of whom married for the first time, registered in China and practiced for real the nation's quintessential ritual in their motherland. Though one of them lived on the other end of the earth away from his ancestors, his interest in hymen was no less than that of his Chinese compatriots. The other, trying hard to pretend to be a virgin, coyly and admiringly presented a pantomime in which she fought against her enemy without reservation, but all of a sudden an unchecked bold moan gave away her true feelings. Gravely misguided by Hollywood movies, Xiang An thought that no American would pigheadedly quibble over the issue of virginity like Luo Ke, unaware that a Chinese ethics course introduced by a Chinese American had arrived from across the ocean. It was conceivable that studying this course on her own would be Xiang An's lifelong homework—like each meal in Tang Dynasty consisting of American ingredients and Chinese culinary arts, nothing was missed and everything was exquisite. But when engagement banquet ended, the relatives already started talking behind her back, as if her body had changed overnight. For the first time Xiang An felt that the die was cast. The classical tragedy of a Chinese woman had to be continued when they moved to the United States of America. Besides, Xiang An had been looking forward to the United States, and therefore she could only grin and bear it even if she would go through the harshest trials. In a suite at a three-star hotel, Xiang An sobbed late into the night. Her beauty made Mr. Ma anxious. Every inch of her skin was clearly made by another pair of hands. Richard Ma made love with her, though jealous in mood, and comforted her while trampling on her. Xiang An felt pleased, disgusted, wronged and resentful. They had one thing in common, the expectation for the day when they felt indifferent to come early, or the day when they could break up as dramatically as water splashing into a hot pan of oil.

3

As was set up by fate beforehand, Luo Ke willingly walked into the trap after roaming for a while. Ten to two in the afternoon, driven by the call from Zhu Ke, he went to revisit an old place. He parked the dirty and old bicycle in the dark corridor on the ground floor of the Xicun Apartment and forgot to lock it in haste. He walked up the stairs step by step around the rusty lift in the middle of the building which had stopped operating for long. It appeared that the westernized apartment building was renovated once during the post-completion years, but now the original earth yellow under the grass green painted afterwards had been mercilessly exposed. It was as gross and confusing as mud coming out of cabbage. The hazy light and shadows, the funk of the wet old wood and the metallic smell of the rusty lift frame—everything suddenly aroused Luo Ke's mixed feelings. He himself did not understand why as soon as he detected the smell of an old house, he would feel compassion and stand in utter awe toward those unintelligible words like vicissitudes, thinking of those dead men completely unrelated to himself—Arabs who lost their way and died in desert, philosophers who died a natural death, nameless bodies on an ancient battlefield, people who ran away from home, people who went missing in broad day light, people who denied themselves and disappeared, people who shone in biographies, people who appeared in your life and bid farewell in your dream, deceased great figures, villains who were fondly remembered, the dumb who kept silent with no regret even when nearing death, people who kept talking rubbish in their life, cautious people who died a sudden death, people who failed in trying to die and finally became stones in one piece, people who died for love, people who died for defending a concept, people who died when they were born (Stillborn babies!), the immortal and the living dead. In the very doorway next to Yin Mang's house, a man in a vegetative state was being cared for, which cost a fortune. At this very moment Luo Ke was walking past his (Its?) door.

When Luo Ke was just about to press the milky white spot on the doorbell of Yin Mang's flat, the door on the other side opened. The afternoon sunlight shone into the corridor, and then (What a fate!) a pale, wrinkled, fragrant, feminine face of a man appeared with backlighting.

Luo Ke grit his teeth, fists tight, while thinking that it was time for some serious reflection. Why did he always appeal to homosexuals? Was the odds of meeting the same feminine man twice in ten years in a big city with millions of people above or matching the average probability? Or was he unaware that he himself was a potential homosexual?

"Mr. Gao!" Luo Ke had no choice but to call him. The eternal greeting sent him back to those disgusting biology classes in the high school. Pale but gentle, Mr. Gao hid his face in the shadow and said with an affected tone, "It's great to see you! You hadn't come to visit me all these years after graduation ..." Luo Ke interrupted him, "I didn't know that you live here." "Ah, then why are you here?" Again, Luo Ke recollected Mr. Gao guiding students to play with a medical manikin marked with acupuncture points. His fingers covered by chalk dust caressed all over the one-foot tall man made of enamel, his expression as satisfied as that of an infant taking milk.

"I've come to visit a friend."

"Girlfriend!" Mr. Gao smiled understandingly, "There were several daughters in that family, though none of them was at home. One in jail, one went abroad ..." He took the echoing corridor as his classroom, extending the subject on his own.

"I'll come another day." The moment Luo Ke, who was dying to flee, turned around, Mr. Gao grabbed his arm, "What's the hurry? Come and sit for a while in my room! There's no reason to leave since you have come by my house." Luo Ke could not be more familiar with that force. In the inner room of the biology office piled with teaching aids, among the glass cabinets with hanging spider webs and the same musty smell, it was this hand that unbuckled the military belt that Luo Ke was proud of (Oh, where is it now?).

"No!" Luo Ke removed that persistent, audacious, sweaty hand with the hand that had carried cannonballs, "Go unbuckle your own belt." Luo Ke ran downstairs and home nonstop. Of course, when he went back to the Xicun Apartment, his bicycle was gone.

4

For a woman who was about to set out on a journey, nothing was more annoying than selecting belongings. You could certainly compare a purse to an exquisite, compact suitcase, clean yet also messy inside, as if a demonic shelter. Liu Yazhi, abiding by women's interests, threw everything indispensable, such as a small handkerchief, a small toothbrush, small nail clippers, a small compact, and a small round mirror, into the brown faux leather travel bag. Later when she wanted to check if she missed anything, those little things had long been jumbled up with an unopened package of silk stocking, a washed underwear, absorbent paper, several letters from home, one or two novels, gum, comic-book-style photo albums, keys connected by four or five little iron rings, folded travel guides, and a silk scarf.

When Luo Ke came in, Liu Yazhi was kneeling down before the travel bag as if kowtowing, her left hand pressing the ground and right hand stirring in the bag. She was concentrated and somewhat impatient, as if catching fish in a small pond.

"What are you looking for?"

"I forgot where I put my ferry ticket. Get some water for yourself."

The room was in a shambles, like an exhibit hall ready to be dismantled after the exhibition ended. Everything was put where it was not supposed to be.

"Are you going to transport all the junk to Macau?"

"No, my relatives will come and take them in a while."

"What about these paintings?"

"Burn them as free fuel."

Those good landscape facsimiles were randomly stacked up in a corner of the room, presenting the lonely scenery of the French countryside over a century ago. Luo Ke realized that she was truly leaving and not coming back. When someone abandoned her hobby which had lasted half her life, she was probably undergoing some veritable transformation. He felt that he had anticipated everything, as if he had experienced this situation in the mists of the past. Maybe everything would happen twice, once in the unidentifiable memory, once on the spot when the memory was evoked.

"It seems that I have seen this day coming," Luo Ke pretended to blurt, trying to find something to say.

"Don't say such things. To live by hunches does great harm to your physical and mental health." She finally found the ferry ticket, squinting at it for quite a while in such a satisfied manner as if she were reading a bank check. She looked one or two years younger in a light gray sport suit, her hair just washed, with a delicate scent of perfume under the earlobe. She walked around in the room, lifting everything up to take a look and mumbling the name of each object. Luo Ke thought that there was nothing for them to talk about.

In some transient moment, Luo Ke desperately hoped that he was a glib man, who could probably manage to help people through difficult times just by talking ceaselessly. Luo Ke looked at the woman who was only a step away from him, those happy scenarios which would never return emerging before his eyes, as if he were mourning an episode which would soon be buried by sand, mud and leaves of space and state border. And the grave of this affair would float to the depths of his heart, which would always keep it, and sleep there for eternity, like the chatter of a streak of time with the blow of sorrow.

As night fell, the sounds of the day outside the window died away.

"Do you want to turn on the light?" Liu Yazhi asked in darkness.

"You might as well take the bulb off."

Like this, Liu Yazhi and Luo Ke sat next to each other on a roll of carpet.

"Are you hungry?" Liu Yazhi suddenly asked, after some time.

"Do you have any other relatives in Macau, apart from your mother?"

"I think I will, as long as I marry someone again. But I won't." She turned her head toward Luo Ke and smiled.

"Will we keep in touch?" Luo Ke asked.

"I don't know."

"Yeah," Luo Ke thought, "except what had just happened, what do we know?" The sky took away its last light, and the outlines of furniture and luggage merged into darkness. Liu Yazhi suddenly put her hand on Luo Ke's palm. The familiar and peaceful feeling of a woman's body temperature swept away his flickering desire. The relationship between Luo Ke and Liu Yazhi was changed by the gentle touch of their palms. It was a pure farewell handshake, whose warmth contained a little wetness, like the chilly warmth of a kiss goodbye left on the forehead.

5

Luo Ke,

Sorry that it took me so long to write to you. I always defended myself by saying that I hadn't promised to write to you, but it was that excuse that made me feel that I should write to you. But this might be the only letter I'll ever write. Even at this moment I do not know why I'm going to tell you my story. I'll tell you what, no one except my ex-husband and doctor knows this. Of course, it is also the reason he divorced me. I'm infertile. I have no pleasure in sex and have to feign the reaction that a woman could possibly have. What happened in the summer when I was seventeen years old only accounted for part of it. Later I went to an army farm in the northern wilderness with many people. That winter I fell in the paddy field during menstruation. After that I suffered from menstrual disorder and my lower limbs were always cold. God knows how much medicine I took, but it never worked. I felt hopeless. Afterwards my sexual life became a mess, but it did not solve the problem. My womb is cold, which can never be changed in this life. I tell you this only because I do not want to cheat you. I guess you were only a child when you met me. Please forgive me. I didn't do that because I felt happy, but because I wanted to feel happy. You mistook my misery for happiness that you gave me, which made me upset. I can hardly imagine you as morbid as my husband. After all, sex is what I desire, and that desire has made me drift away from you and him.

Let's say goodbye.

I'm really sorry.

Yazhi at Gubai Road in Macau

6

It was not long before Liu Yazhi sent Luo Ke another letter—a lengthy one on a scented, light blue piece of paper. Every trivial matter in her life was arranged on the paper in the order of the degree of interest. She briefed him on her mother's condition, and then mentioned her new boyfriend. "He is quite smart." There seemed to be a little helplessness in her admiration for his smartness. Apart from that, she told Luo Ke that through the local newspapers, she came to know many things unknown to the mainland, but then unexpectedly wrote "no politics" on purpose. At the end of the letter, she wrote some sentimental words to imply that she was touched by their memories.

Luo Ke held the letter with two fingers, legs rested on the desk in front of him, thinking leisurely. Liu Yazhi's tragic (but not necessarily not hedonistic) migration gave him room for the taste of writing, which had been suppressed before. Luo Ke always considered his literary dream part of his basic needs, just like the need for tasty food. But basic needs (sometimes even craving) would not lead him to rack his brains to open a restaurant; at best he would browse through his greasy cookbook.

Like a cheat who had plotted for a long time, Luo Ke was going to write about his cousin Tao Lie's story in an autobiographical (Rapacious?) approach, which was commonly adopted in the history of literature. Before writing, he imagined how those prolific contemporaries like Zhu Ke would criticize this ridiculous story and dig out some profound meanings which was probably not even contained in the story itself. He had a name in mind for this future novel, *The Screen*, which came from the screen that Tao Lie dragged everywhere. He would portray those assorted characters, whose life revolved around the screen, and wrote about their partings and reunions, through the lost-and-found-and-lost-again cycle of the object (Not a human!). For example: (Luo Ke thought complacently) after Tao Lie died, Aunt Tao Bo'er (of course, she needed another name) finally found the screen after some twists and turns. But in 1966 (Vicissitudes in life!), the Red Guards confiscated it. And after 1976 (Aren't these periods specifically chosen as some symbols, or metaphors?), this item alone (which was indispensable in the story) was missing in the property returned. Therefore, Luo Yizhi (Sorry, dad!) spared no efforts to search for it everywhere and finally (another finally) found it accidentally (What a trick life had played on him!) in someone's house, when he was almost about to give up. And this person had to be involved in a long feud with Luo's family. (Well, who?) This time, the price of rosewood furniture soared (Oh, money!), and according to an expert, the phoenixes on the screen were carved by a well-known craftsman in the period of late Ming Dynasty (1368–1644) and early Qing Dynasty (1644–1911). Hence the story entered another stage. It seemed that it was to be perfectly finished, and those unexpected turns made the story of the screen accord with the law that a fiction consists of twisted stories, allowing readers to see people and their fate and times of transition through one object. In short, writing about that piece of furniture was equivalent to writing about history. And also, he needed to check a dictionary, copy the content under the "screen" entry with some adaptations in his novel, and go to a consignment store to acquire some knowledge about rosewood furniture. As a result, the book would appear to have more learning and deep knowledge of traditional customs and would also become more readable. As for those things beyond his reach, just write ambiguously. In this way, personal incompetence would be in parallel with the world as a maze. But, wait, how embarrassing is that! Aunt Tao Bo'er wouldn't forgive me in the first place. Luo Ke mused that though her adopted son died of a filthy disease, she would jump and slap one in the face if one dared to show a bit of contempt in front of her. Plus, this kind of story is interesting to read but might be extremely boring to make up. Who knows? Liu Yazhi is right. It's not my thing.

"What are you mumbling in your mouth there?" Luo Yizhi asked Luo Ke, craning his neck into the room and raising his glasses, "If you still don't go to work, they are going to fire you."

7

Autumn came. Night fell on the city in a drizzle. The streetlight gave off a dim light, glowing in loneliness, as if only to illuminate the autumn rain. Its limited radiance was seldom endowed with the poetic beauty that poets often discovered in nature itself or in their heart. The monotonous and cold light contained a contemporary, dull, lasting and disastrous emotion. In every night of stillness, Luo Ke would be agitated by the sounds in darkness. A word or two from pedestrians in the distance, a clear clink of windows in the gentle night breeze, a moan of her mother in sleep in the adjacent room and the sound of the earliest milkman pulling his cart at around two o'clock—these all became the music of a sleepless night and the knock on the door of memory with the mallet of reflection. Several minutes ago, Luo Ke was in the pitch-black corridor, listening to the dull footsteps of Xiang An walking downstairs, which, when she walked out of the building, were finally engulfed by the stillness studded by the patter of rain. When they said goodbye in darkness, both were no longer interested in extending their hands to each other. It was as if they had lost interest in even leafing through a book that they had learnt by heart. This was a book whose cover was bestrewn with wrinkles caused by touching, with worn out edges, personal comments in the margins, some pages accidentally torn off, lines drawn every time with excited understanding in innumerable times of reading to show full comprehension, an unchangeable background presented on the copyright page, dedication on the first page, and a synopsis on the back cover which allowed a quick grasp of its content. He did not know whether it would be put on the shelf of romance. If one still wanted to read, one could only hope for a reprint, as this copy could not stand to be finished anyway.

The moment Luo Ke opened the door, he tried to figure out the reason Xiang An came. "I don't want to explain." Unprepared, he started listening to an explanation of not wanting to explain. But the following conversation was spaced by a succession of pauses, like a play by Harold Pinter. "I don't know where to start," she said. "Let me give you a piece of advice. Just start form 'I don't know where to start.'" Suddenly Luo Ke did not feel any aversion and prepared himself to intertwine repentance, guilt, apology, a sense of loss, a review of expectation and pure rhetoric into the conversation. "We know each other too well." Luo Ke thought the implication of this pair of assertion would be "We don't know each other well." "Forget it," Xiang An suddenly stopped continuing the topic, "I've come just to say goodbye." "Then you should go now." Seeing how indifferent he was, Luo Ke asked himself whether it was a mistake, a generous abandonment of fury.

Xiang An's painstaking rehearsal of her farewell on a rainy right was almost in vain. She simply gave up words and became silent. Then, crying, accompanied by spasms and trembles, rolled in like thunder accompanied by lightning. Luo Ke also kept silent along with her at first, but when Xiang An's emotional tears poured out of her eyes, he terminated his accompanying silence. He knew that once he comforted her and showed his understanding, he would not be able to avoid the last ritual-like farewell ... He could not find an appropriate word to describe the potential sex. He saw that weird scene through her sobbing and exhalation. "Let it go," Luo Ke told himself, "and don't do things you could not express or describe."

8

The next morning, the ceaseless autumn rain continued to fall. In the damp air with a hint of sourness, the rain made a few fallen plane leaves stick to the pavement. Those leaves, which indicated the change of seasons, were of different shades and similar shapes, and their sparse embellishment of the streets gave an imperceptible air of decadence to this southern city.

Luo Ke walked slowly in the rain with an old-fashioned black umbrella in his hand. Though sleep deprivation made him look obtuse, he still managed to notice that the chilly autumn rain secretly connected certain things wide apart. When he arrived at the Xicun Apartment, the rain was easing. Two sodden sparrows walked out of the gate, unfazed. They met Luo Ke, fluttered their wings and flew up to the electric wires where the water drops were hanging, as if they were not willing to greet him. Luo Ke ignored those two pecking little things, quickened his pace and walked directly to Yin Mang's door. He leaned sideways and listened to the sounds inside, trying to use his ear to reproduce the situation in the house with the door as a partition. It was quiet inside. He could not hear the sound of people walking or talking, and the quietness even dislodged the furniture. He pressed the bell. Nothing responded but the echoes of emptiness. He rapped on the door with his palm, and the sound immediately echoed in the whole building.

"Who are you looking for?" a hoarse woman's voice behind him asked.

Luo Ke recognized this young woman with short hair. "I know you." He heard himself almost yelling in the corridor. "I also recognized you," she said, pulling out her key and inserting it in the keyhole. "You used to wear a ponytail." "I did before going to prison. Do you want to stand here or come inside?" Luo Ke raised his umbrella and pointed inside. "OK." She went into the room before him.

Luo Ke walked across the passage and stood where Yin Mang's seventh brother played cello. In the kitchen, there was nothing but a sofa covered with dust, an old wardrobe, a chair lying on the ground, white chrysanthemums long dead in a box on the windowsill, and light colored curtains taken off and piled in the corner.

"Yin Mang went to Australia half a year ago." That hoarse voice came up again behind Luo Ke. She poured a glass of boiled water for herself, sipping at it.

"I came to ask about her situation. I heard that …"

"You are not in contact? You didn't call her?"

"No." Luo Ke wanted to explain the whole thing, but he held back the words when they came to the tip of his tongue, "I know that you are Yin Mang's second sister, but I don't know your name."

"Just call me Second Sister. It's easier," she said, turning back to the kitchen and pouring another glass of water for herself. "But I didn't hear from Yin Mang, either. She never wrote to me. What else do you want to know?" She crossed her feet, making a dancing posture, as if she had just came back from her gym class.

"You live here alone?" Luo Ke asked with a tone of a weather forecaster, afraid that she might misunderstand him.

"They all moved away, and sold the furniture. The house doesn't belong to me. I have to move, too," she said, finishing her second glass of water. She put the glass on the top of the cupboard, walked across the passage, and opened the door for Luo Ke. "Please." With a pause, she added, "I'm on medical parole."

Luo Ke had to pick up that dripping umbrella and walked toward the door. Passing the door of the inner room, he saw a rosewood screen standing beside the door. The unexpected discovery instantly refreshed him.

"May I ask?"

"No. As a man you have too many questions." Before closing the door, "Second Sister" enlightened Luo Ke through the gap, "A woman asks one question while thinking of ten. A man should think of ten questions and then ask one."

9

As Yin Mang's father, an outstanding railway engineer and husband of three unfortunate wives, Yin Dongshan, who was always running around, had experienced what could be called a rough life. The traces of his miserable life could still be vaguely seen in his belongings left behind. In a notebook with a satin cover, nearly a hundred classical poems with simple phrasing but obscure meanings were written down in beautiful handwriting. There were refined metaphors, far-fetched allusions to classics, crazy and mechanical application of some idioms and vernacular chitchat everywhere. The most astonishing part was that every several pages there was a loud cry from the torment of jealousy. These twisted poems revealed incompletely the lamentable and uncanny misfortunes of his first two wives. Those past stories of unspeakable suffering proceeded intermittently in the works of the classical poet Yin Dongshan, sometimes visible but sometimes not. In that summer (it seemed to be a day in early autumn in another five-character octave), a woman (his first wife), who was compared to a water lily, died horribly under a tramcar, wheels sparking on the track when the emergency brake was applied. The traffic accident was planned beforehand, which could be proved by a row of pedicab drivers who were then taking a break by the road. "That driver went nuts," they said categorically. The driver was "water lily's" lover. The poet did not know why he murdered his wife, as the affair was not exposed before the atrocious act. The railway engineer imagined the mutilated body of his beloved wife lying on the track. Sometimes with tinkling sounds, the scene, where the driver and his wife stood next to each other and enjoyed the sight of the streets on the tramcar rumbling forward, would replace the scene of the dead body at the entrance of the Sweet Love Park.

With several pages skipped, following a sentimental group poem, his second wife, who was also referred to as a water lily, strolled in the rhythm which gradually grew mature. In an archaic tone Water Lily II was playing the piano, the slender fingers moving up and down fast. Her amiable and lovely mien, with the white keys undulating like waves and the black keys gliding like seagulls, formed a splendid picture as touching as sunset. She sat still in the half-light by the window at dusk, as if being moved by the past and reminiscence. She was on Yin Dongshan's side for most of the happy times of his life. Her character was impeccable. She was a stepmother with few words, who always appeared unnoticeably and then disappeared quietly. She was always wearing a meditative look of a bystander. All of these came into Yin Dongshan's life, as well as his poems. But she also failed to escape from the shadow of death. Which year was it (the poet asked in his poem)? She killed herself by jumping off a disused lift shaft, holding tightly to her Persian cat. She picked a stormy night, and in a rumbling her taciturn life was taken to the netherworld. That Persian cat, its fur as shiny as satin, survived. But what could people expect it to say? In those poems which grew more and more solemn, there was no record of the year in which Water Lily II died. What was just as puzzling was that there was no reason for it, either. There was only a location: the old lift shaft which was compared to a "valley." Maybe as far as death was concerned, the location was the only fatal factor, while time and means were only props randomly chosen.

Though the railway engineer's poems showed that he was a sentimental man, he was not daunted by the horrible scenes of death one after another, and was still devoted to the vortex of marriage as ever. Once he encouraged his many sons in a letter sent home from the campsite on an exploratory trip in the wild, "If death was only to scare away our passion for marriage, then death ceased to exist a long time ago."

10

When Luo Ke came in, Luo Yizhi was hunching over the desk by the window, writing quickly. His memoir had reached his school days. Judging from the look on his face at the moment, he was in a light mood. His pen was scribbling on a landscape of his hometown, sparing no efforts to revive a small town in a basin over half a century ago, eliciting sounds from the rivers and mountains kept in his memory. He mumbled, ejecting heavy breath onto the manuscript, as if the magic breath could bring the characters in the book back to life.

Luo Ke walked around the desk several times and saw that his father was still absorbed in writing. He could only settle down on the sofa and wait for him to drop the pen when he met a block. He reached out his hand, grabbed the *Ancient and Contemporary Stories* on the tea table and started browsing. He leafed through the pages back and forth, as if looking for a mistake in the bookbinding. Suddenly he buried his head into the open book, immersing himself in the mixed fragrance of paper and ink. At last he clapped the book on the desk, rose to his feet and headed for the door. "Please call me when you take a break." "Stop!" Luo Yizhi said in a sonorous, invigorated voice, lifting his head from the autobiography, "Son, may I ask who you were talking to?"

"Sorry, dad. I didn't mean to offend you." Luo Ke heard himself coaxing his father in an evasively low voice.

"I never thought a young man like you would apologize." Though the old playwright was irritated, his son's rare humble attitude, which had taken a sudden turn, was like iced lemonade pouring into his burning throat, moistening the vocal cords.

"I want to borrow three thousand." Luo Ke grasped the opportunity and cut to the chase.

"What for?" Luo Ke's motive for playing a filial son was unmasked in a second by himself, but Luo Yizhi's anger was still calmed down by the affection aroused by his son's words (Lines?). He sat in the sofa next to the desk, lying on his back, and started to put tobacco shreds in the pipe.

"To buy something." Luo Ke's voice turned towards that of a disobedient son.

"What?"

"Are you going to give it to me or not?" Now Luo Ke was playing an armed robber.

"Have you come to me to borrow the money or just to draw it?" The old man looked at his son who was provoked by him, delighted to experience again the satisfaction of manipulating those actors running lines in the rehearsal hall in the past. "State your reason, and you can draw the money immediately." The playwright succinctly clarified the price for getting the money.

"To buy something."

"You have just said that. To buy what exactly?" I have just said that too, Luo Yizhi thought.

"A screen," Luo Ke coughed out a key word.

Luo Yizhi barely heard what Luo Ke said, but his aim was achieved. He went back to the writing desk, examined the pile of kraft envelopes in the drawer for quite a while and pulled out one of them. He took a stack of fifties out of it, counted out sixty and put them on the desk.

"You should learn from foreigners. They don't take money from their old men."

"Says who? Foreigners kill their old men for money." Luo Ke grabbed the money on the desk and rushed outside like a gust of wind.

Luo Yizhi was still outspoken at last. He heaved a sigh and went back again to his hometown which was growing more and more tender and loveable in his autobiography.

11

The twelfth sister's number was 9876 when she served time in prison, and it became 54 when she was on medical parole. Her father, the miserable poet and upbeat railway engineer, chose "Yin Chu" as her name.

To herself, there was nothing special about the name. She'd

rather that people call her the twelfth sister, second sister or something like that. An African friend of hers, who brought her misfortune, called her *tuwei'er* (bunny's tail, similar to twelve in pronunciation) at one time. Normally, Yin Chu never cared whether people called her bunny's tail or dog's tail. She had been a giggly optimist since childhood, who only occasionally cried while in trouble and would soon recover after she blew her nose and washed her face.

If one asked Yin Chu to think of her childhood, her reply would be clear-cut, "boring." If one made further inquiries like a policeman, she would begin to equivocate, uttering modal particles like a series of ohs. Yin Chu was born a clique activist. From kindergarten to middle school she was always surrounded by a group of boys and girls who followed her like a shadow. They ganged up to make trouble, which was nothing more than children's pranks. Yin Chu's talent for mischief was slightly more outstanding than her ability to deal with schoolwork. For quite a long time she was considered a potential juvenile delinquent by her teacher in chief. (Unfortunately the prediction was confirmed by Yin Chu's own action.)

Yin Chu's life after she left school was even harder to describe. Apart from that she still had many friends with dubious backgrounds as before, her beautiful face and flowery dress transformed her from a so-called innocent girl to a vixen who smoked and drank. When she smiled and wrinkled her nose as something good happened, there was still a trace of angelic goodness to be found on the lifted corners of her mouth, at other times she was mostly an overburdened theologian.

Yin Chu had always liked her father, but there were fewer and fewer conversations between the father and the daughter. Sometimes she would complain to Yin Mang, "I really don't get what old people are thinking all day." Besides, she always grumbled that their house was like the lobby of an auditorium, which was clamorous with people coming and going. Yin Chu's most famous comment on her family was "a monotonous scene."

She always emphasized that she was responsible for the family. In that respect she was not like other children who had their own way and brushed family aside as long as they were having fun. She was resolved to save the family which was falling apart. This resolution of hers was made in front of a jail officer when she heard the bad news about his father.

Relatively speaking, the degree of intimacy between Yin Chu and Yin Mang was only second to that with their romantic and perseverant father. They often discussed certain moral issues, such as whether they should tell everything to their father no matter how important or how trivial, whether concealment equaled deceit, whether telling a lie occasionally was good for the healthy development of consciousness, etc. But the result of their discussion depended, and the conclusion of this week was often contrary to that of last week. If Yin Mang was a learned woman, Yin Chu was a clever one, and one could get a sense of it from her unique explanation of music appreciation. Once in a winter vacation, she was inspired by the divine line of W. J. Smith Yin Mang copied on her notebook, "The lights at the lover's school are out," and expounded on how the misery in darkness and the confusion which was hard to express needed not light but stroking. She then said that darkness was transparent in music, and that listeners did not have to watch as long as they were conscious. But she did not remember whether these explanations had also come from Yin Mang's notebook.

Yin Chu's first boyfriend was her classmate. She cherished her first love. During the time they spent together, they were either studying the meaning of love with an adult-like language or kissing and fondling each other. When night fell and they had to go home, they would imitate people in movies, repeatedly turning around to show their reluctance to separate until one of them disappeared around the corner and the other into darkness. The great time at night was exclusively for concocting love letters which they would exchange the next day. Yin Chu would spread a piece of light pink writing paper on the desk and drag her galloping thoughts into the river of love. In a while, rows of sweet, soft words of love would appear on the paper, interspersed with all kinds of nicknames like big fool, little idiot, sweetheart, caterpillar, giant, bass … Seeing her feelings flowing from the pen, Yin Chu was so delighted that she could not help wagging her head. Her boyfriend, dubbed the king of love letters in his school, was a master who excelled in suiting his methods to the situation. He was used to making a stew of hearsay, headlines in newspapers and magazines, paradigms in classics and his own love letters in earlier days, blending and infusing them into a girl's heart. This romantic episode did not end until Yin Chu appreciated a batch of similar works in her girl deskmate's hand.

Perhaps Yin Chu inherited from her father the grittiness and composure. She said goodbye to her first love in haste, turned around and threw herself into a succession of relationships. These whirling, dizzying life-and-death romances overlapped each other in different fields. Her lovers came from all walks of life, including a pediatrician, a truck driver, a nameless poet at university, a grain store man … Finally one day, when she was resting in bed after an abortion, she felt great fatigue and pain, as if battered and scarred. It occurred to her that these short and messy relationships were only games in love's clothing. On the surface it was like a certain lifestyle, but in fact it was more like self-abandon in terms of feelings. Yin Chu picked a day when there was no one at home and cried out loud alone. With her nose running and tears streaming down her face, she walked around in every room—she blew her nose in the bathroom, poured a glass of water in the kitchen, peeped outside when she walked past the living room, opened the fridge and took a look inside. At last, she opened her wardrobe and took out her clothes, reorganizing them one by one, which soothed her grief beyond verbal expression. The chaos of relationships in Yin Chu's personal history took about ten years. She realized that she had barely done anything else since she walked out of high school. "Not f--king worthwhile," she commented on the ten chaotic years of her own.

12

On the whole, Luo Ke was not one of those who deliberated over things, though there were quite a few weird thoughts in his mind. He was used to being dragged by these fragmentary cloud-like scraps instead of synthesizing, summarizing or organizing them. Carrying the free loan which he cheated his father out of, he walked along the pavement in front of the Xicun Apartment back and forth, like a fledgling spy who was waiting to exchange intel. Yin Chu, who was required to appear according to his plan, did not show up. He could only picture again and again that screen, which was up for sale, gradually being covered by dust. On the rooftop of the Xicun Apartment stood arrays of television antennas of different shapes, above which white clouds were floating by at the moment. The azure blue sky, compared with the morning three days ago with low-hanging dark clouds and patter of rain, was satisfactorily agreeable. Luo Ke, who was walking slowly, did not feel anxious or impatient. One of the reasons he chose to wait was to kill time, but a more important, and also more obscure one was that he was afraid of meeting that retired biology teacher again. The yearning for the screen and praying that he could be spared from meeting Mr. Gao became Luo Ke's spell. One moment he saw the cleaned shiny screen before his eyes, the next moment he glimpsed Mr. Gao pop up in front of Luo Ke, the furniture collector who was elated as if stoned, and blocked his way in an imposing manner. In Luo Ke's memory which was hard to erase, Mr. Gao was truly an exceptional man who remained aloof from the world. He made no attempt to disguise the way he held the teaching aids and books as if holding a silk handkerchief, and walked on the playground and hallways on campus with the small steps of a female character in Peking Opera. He smiled like a lady by holding his chin back when talking reservedly with those young soccer players who soon disappeared. The intimacy between him and the women teachers he mixed with reminded Luo Ke of those househusbands who were good at housekeeping, while the dandruff which could never be whisked off the shoulders of his jacket made his image shift towards a middle-aged man who preferred celibacy. And his melodious chirping when he sang loud in the staff chorus gave healthy clothing of the ancient Mediterranean style to his homosexual inclination. Despite that, Mr. Gao still married a homely, kind-hearted weaver at the age of forty. It took less than a year for this wife with a big mouth to give birth to a baby boy weighing 1.85 kilograms. His pet name was Axiong (*xiong* means male), which more or less suggested Mr. Gao's complicated and subtle ambition of masculinity. Three years later when Luo Ke was about to graduate from high school, the child began to develop and show his traits. Gao Axiong literally became a mini replica of his father. Every gesture of his indicated that he naturally understood the secret held in Mr. Gao's heart. His father held him like a loving mother and walked among the desks and chairs in every staff room, showing his male and female colleagues his personal work. Gao Axiong was delighted to meet people, always grinning, and the saliva streamed all the way down his cheek and stuck on his father's chest. Mr. Gao took off the child's handkerchief tucked under his son's chin and cleaned himself up with ease, completely unembarrassed. At last the father and son came to Luo Ke, monitor of the biology class, who was holding a stack of homework. "Call him uncle, Axiong. Call him! Call Uncle." Luo Ke looked at the masterpiece of heredity with all sorts of feelings welling up in his heart. "No, don't push him. He can call me when he grows up." "When he grows up?"

The father calculated seriously, "When he grows up I'm afraid you won't have the opportunity to meet him." It was almost noon. The sky grew clearer and the warm sun climbed above his head. Luo Ke was bored and pulled back his thoughts from memory and faced the situation at hand like an agent whose mind had just been wandering. The crowded vehicles were diluted at lunchtime, thinly scattered on the road. The drivers were cheered up because they could push down hard on the accelerator or because their stomach sensed the smell of lunch. As for those who were driving slowly, they must have had a bargain lunch somewhere early. Watching this scene, Luo Ke, whose empty stomach was rumbling, had to cancel this purely business-related stakeout. He touched his chest to see if the money was still there, turned around and went back home.

13

Luo Ke strode westward along the avenue, praying to Jesus or Sakyamuni or Mohammed or just anyone of them for epiphany, which would allow him to meet Yin Chu before he turned the corner onto another road. While he kept mumbling, turning north in despair, he heard a burst of laughter from the traffic booth. Luo Ke turned back and saw Yin Chu talking in a brotherly manner with a traffic policeman whose face was tanned and glowing. The automatic traffic signal blinked its eyes with clicks on the street corner, and the young traffic policeman scanned around with his sharp eyes from time to time. Luo Ke walked up to them and stuck his head into the booth. "Excuse me, could you tell me the way to the Xicun Apartment?"

"Why, Luo Ke? What are you doing? I saw you stand for half a day in front of our apartment, and now you come here to ask where the Xicun Apartment is?"

"Who's this?" asked the traffic policeman seriously.

"Oh, he's with me." Yin Chu explained in a formal manner, "Let me introduce you to each other. This is my former classmate. This one, well, to be honest, has a complicated background." She finished and jumped out of the booth.

"Have you come to see me?"

"What did you mean by I'm with you?" Luo Ke asked, panting.

"Well, I meant ... Don't take it seriously. You are quite sensitive. How come Yin Mang fell in love with such a childish guy like you?"

"All right, all right. Seriously, you've got some furniture to sell, right? This is what I've come to you for," said Luo Ke.

"Aha, I didn't see that you are a junk dealer. Fine, what do you want? That pair of leather sofas? They are pretty good stuff, just a little worn, but the style is authentically German."

"No, not the sofas. I want that screen."

"Screen?" Yin Chu eyed Luo Ke suspiciously, "What screen? How come I didn't know there was a screen in our house? Where is it?"

"Your eyes are big for nothing. Beside the door of the north-facing room across the corridor. It's leaned up against the wall."

"Whose eyes are big for nothing? You think that's a screen? That's a door we removed when we were moving furniture."

"Don't fool me," Luo Ke murmured.

"You really want that door?" Yin Chu took a step towards Luo Ke, "Is that an excuse?"

"Is love included in the other ten questions?" Luo Ke remembered Yin Chu's one to ten theory of men and women's ways of asking questions.

"Do you have nine questions left or have you thought about the ten questions including love?" asked Yin Chu.

"All questions boil down to one," Luo Ke said.

"Yin Mang always said that, too. It's so boring."

"Are you going to sell it or not?"

"Oh, that door again." Yin Chu started laughing.

14

Luo Ke had always told himself candidly, "You were a lovelorn man." The girl he deeply loved, who no longer loved him, left him a comment: neurotic. Luo Ke came to understand that ancient and pallid (Pathologically?) definition, love was a sickness. Even nowadays, people could easily gain authoritativeness by using medical terms to describe things, as if your handbag were filled with amphetamine, Corydrane (a Benzedrine drug), barbiturates (a sedative) and Atropine. If Luo Ke was still trying to be a writer, (he tried reading them aloud, which sounded like demonic pronunciation), he would have to use these things alternately, or at least talk about them profusely, in order to indulge himself in chaos and despair. Like Sartre after forty.

There was a general psychoanalytic view that success (Please read repeatedly until being satisfied, thought Luo Ke.) could help avoid and partly cure all sorts of psychosis. A strong supporter of the cultural determinism was Karen Horney. Of course, no one would pursue failure. Further, no one could pursue failure successfully. That was a relatively more complete formulation. Except those incurable patients.

Luo Ke thought there were some rumor-like remarks spread in a certain area of the world after Yin Mang abandoned him. According to those ambiguous expressions in different combinations, Luo Ke, who dreamed of becoming a writer, had some secret interests like that of Oscar Wilde and Andre Gide. Luo Ke had to admit (at least in theory) that everyone was a potential homosexual. But this kind of in-between attitude did not indicate that he would yield to anyone's verbal violence.

Luo Ke was extremely fragile. For example, when people talked about wanting to cower, he would think of impotence.

When people talked about continuing the revolution, he would think of exploration, failure, a second exploration, a second failure, until destruction. He needed salvation, which came from Jesus, who was born in the manger. Both his humility and shyness was refreshing to Luo Ke.

Luo Ke was still attached to Yin Mang, who was the only woman that had read the Old Testament to him. Her soft voice wafted gently and brought Luo Ke infinite solace on many nights. Those apostles, martyrs, and authors of the psalms strolled in her reading, with a lethargic look in their eyes and grain in their mouth. Their souls were shining like diamonds.

Her voice was deep and attractive with an enchanting crystalline luster inside. With the saints in the background, it would be reasonable that Luo Ke exaggerated like Heller's David and flattered her throat, vocal cords and the air flowing in and out.

As far as Luo Ke himself was concerned, Yin Mang's reading was the definitive interpretation of the Bible. Its hypnotic effect, its playfulness, as well as her lips full of fine lines and the stains on her teeth were all branded on his mind.

But Luo Ke was abandoned, entirely. One of the opposite sex, a woman, female, feminine, who had some agreement with the tide, constantly followed the moon and could be described as wind and water. Her sex organ was like a celestial body of great mass, which left him with feminine toughness.

Luo Ke imagined beautiful horses meandering on a meadow and envisaged how plants would awaken their appetite and taste when spring came. He wondered whether he would understand their sigh when they smelled the rotten grass roots after galloping.

He knew that her favorite jazz club in the world was in Sidney. It was known for its odd decoration and performance with pretended clumsiness. Once she wrote from the Australian mainland just to tell him that. Luo Ke pictured that when she was watching those musicians playing impromptu, the lifted corners of her mouth still seemed like drooping as it used to.

It was Christmas Eve. The appearance of that western tradition completely unfurled in front of Luo Ke's eyes. There seemed to be warm affection drifting in the chilly air. Countless cards decorated the shop windows with glittering lights in the night, and that famous English word was everywhere to be seen. Girl students, well-dressed women, those young men and people who believed they were still young were looking around in the stores, with their scarves, gloves, red faces, legs trembling under the leather skirt, their exquisite faux leather handbags, gel congealed on the tips of their hair, and their gum which was slightly visible when they grinned. Their cheerfulness constituted an air of warmth which attracted people's attention on the street. Luo Ke also heard music. Someone was singing, with a nasal and hoarse voice. It was sad and romantic, which perfectly suited those nights. A century ago, before they were born, who knew their secret agreement? They were both excited by the ambition of Kemal, the founder of Turkey. On the continental border between Europe and Asia, he said, "We come from the east, and we are going to the west." Yin Mang stared at Luo Ke like Polo, the thirteenth century Venetian, with fantasy, wistfulness and affection in her eyes.

Luo Ke thought this kind of desultory and unvarnished reminiscence probably resembled Heller's so-called self-destructive confession, which at least disturbed himself. Perhaps he should take another more circumlocutory way, just as those who were used to euphemisms translated masturbation into self-consolation in order to cater to the vulgar part of the nature of the young and not so young.

He viewed his life as a long vacation, and indolence was his signature. He took every day as the last day, as if he were something floating between Faust and Don Juan the playboy. He was keen on collecting some astonishing sentences. For example, he excerpted one from Marx's *Economic & Philosophical*

Manuscripts of 1844, "Sex-perception must be the basis of all science."

Luo Ke often told himself that rather than spend time hating a man, he might as well spend the time loving a woman. Though hatred was more lasting than love, he should still pursue the transitory.

When was it that Yin Mang lived in some building in Sidney? Relatively speaking, she was more faraway than Luo Ke from the holy city of Jerusalem. Listening to the love songs on the private radio channel, she cried in the bathroom, cleaning her genitals. She read *Playboy* and the periodical *Diogenes* as well. She called him while sitting next to the bed on the floor, hands between her knees. She said, "This is a different country." To Luo Ke, it sounded like she was talking about another novel (Baldwin!). At last she said, "I love you, honey." It was f--king erotic and distant, he thought.

As Gumilyov said, "I never thought that one could have such love, or feel such grief." To get rid of his misery which might lead to insanity, he took up all the idiotic bad habits. No matter who he met, Luo Ke would try to comfort him or her with a bunch of nonsense, as if the dumb man who had been jilted were not him but someone else. He was fed up with himself, as if he had said something extreme on a public meeting and received attacks from all parties. Disheartened, he returned to his writing full of mannerisms. He sat by the window, eyes bulging towards the sky outside. The look on his face was like that of an animal.

The word mannerism reminded him of Philippe Sollers, who brought him back to 1980. Before he became acquainted with those playboys (he asked himself whether he belonged to them) and fatuously walked into the trap of the so-called bromance, he read Broekman's famous work translated from the 1974 English version published by the Dutch company Reidel. It was Tel Quel that inspired him, hinted his inclination and reminded him of the generativity of language as an accumulation, "Writing does not impart already-existing knowledge ..."

Ten years later he reviewed the small book of one hundred and seventy pages, picturing his literary dream like writing a handbook, as if an index of fate was hidden in the future journey. But it was like a Landolt C chart with broken rings, which all symbolically became "O" in front of Luo Ke's poor eyesight. Just as significantly, zero did not mean that there was nothing, though it could mean emptiness, abyss, or destruction.

As Sollers said, writing was a skill that could only be mastered after numerous mannerisms. Luo Ke thought it was the same as the affairs between lovers, but the problem was that when people were able to naturally express their feelings, they had nothing to express. It was in this way that life separated people.

Luo Ke listened to the music, to an alien language. He dimly felt that both Yin Mang and he would sleep alone. He supposed his thoughts would run wild in his sleep and he would dream of many unique things. The uniqueness that exceeds one. One Thousand and One Nights; one hundred and one rubáiyát of the Persian Khayyam ("Into this Universe, and why not knowing. Nor whence, like Water willy-nilly flowing"). The long separation and endless yearning waited for their destiny to be blown away or buried like footprints on the dunes in a vast desert. He knew that his body would be very quiet, as if Yin Mang's hand were still on his private parts.

But at this moment, who would be playing the harp of her plump body containing the joy of rolling wheat fields in the wind? Would he indulge in her youth and gentleness while resting in her arms, just as he thought for sure in his dream that it was a vessel in paradise?

"Why would I love a man?" He thought, "Like a woman in love." After countless trials, leaving him with keenly-felt pains, Yin Mang was looking at another man with deep affection? Luo Ke did not think of himself as a saint, who could live in stories. Those twisted rumors which were passed on orally could even surpass the brilliance of crystal. Since he was only seeking shelter in reverie, how could he not be hurt by the overwhelming slanders?

Now it was as if the double predicament were making him dance on a blade. The music he chose was narcissistic. But in terms of function, it was just half of Narcissus at most. He looked back to the distant past, his cuffs blotted with ink spots, which were like imaginary ships harbored in the shallow bays of the Apennine Peninsula. At dusk by the Tyrrhenian Sea, the naked men were fighting each other within the vision of Caesar. They were brimming with healthy feelings towards the streets of the ancient state. With blood and speeches, they ran, their private parts slightly hidden and hanging in the Roman wind like a moneybag ... That was Caesar's world before the catastrophe fell upon them, as innocent as Luo Ke's colorless dreamland in his sleep.

15

The Big Strawberry Diner was located on a relatively quiet street in the west of downtown. It would be hard for a customer who only occasionally visited the diner to tell who the owner was, even if he or she sat for quite a while after ordering a cup of hot coffee. People who came in and out of the glass door with a cloth curtain hanging over it were all familiar with each other. If their composed look when greeting each other could be regarded as a sign of being the owner, then normally there would be nearly ten owners scattered in the diner. Outside the glass windows of the Big Strawberry Diner there happened to be a bus station. Every three or five minutes there would come a flurry of noises from the quiet air—the bus braked, three bus doors opened and then closed, the bus started, the conductor shouted at the top of her voice. And after that everything would be quiet again.

The Big Strawberry Diner was a three-in-one synthesis, which not only functioned as a bar and a café but also provided traditional rice topped with other ingredients at any time, which in recent years was referred to by a new name—fast food.

Luo Ke and Yin Chu chose a table next to the wall and sat down. Yin Chu craned her head over the starched white tablecloth, "How about we learn from foreigners and split the bill?"

"Whatever," Luo Ke said.

"To tell you the truth, I never pay the bill when I eat out with a man."

"So you are turning over a new leaf?"

"Perhaps so. What would you like to drink? Luo Ke, I can give you a list of names."

"So can I, but I've never tried any of those things," Luo Ke explained.

"You'd better not. Look at that polished row of bottles. Who knows what they will pour into your glass?"

"I think people who come here to eat are all big fools, like you and me. So be it." Luo Ke opened the plastic card book with a black cover in front of him and pushed it towards Yin Chu. "Read the menu of the Big Strawberry, and pay attention to the footnotes on the right."

"Wow! I can't believe they use this as the menu!"

"Just to follow the market."

A young waiter walked over here with an invoice book under his arm. He was wearing a new shirt, which was white, and around that stiff collar a crinkly, dirty maroon bow tie was superfluously tied. His hair, as shiny as a mirror, was divided in the middle like two cabbage leaves. The young, oily face indicated that he was speculating how much money there was all together in the pockets of Luo Ke and Yin Mang. In a pretended indifferent manner, he said to Yin Mang, "There was nothing below five yuan today (approximately 1 US dollar). What would you like to eat?"

"Have I asked you about anything below five?" Yin Mang

said, as if running the lines with the waiter. He was a little startled and seemed to be choosing a word cautiously, "No."

"Fine. Let me ask you now. Is there anything below five yuan today (she specifically stressed the word)?"

"No," the waiter replied without hesitation.

"All right, we'll come another day then."

Luo Ke and Yin Chu left the waiter and filed out of the Big Strawberry Diner onto the street with bright light. "I thought you didn't care about those things," Luo Ke said in a low voice.

"What?"

"That guy's attitude."

"I care so much. I always pretended that I didn't, but that way it would just be more and more unpleasant." Yin Chu lifted her head and looked into Luo Ke's eyes, "Don't you care?"

"Very much."

16

For the whole summer, Luo Ke stayed with Yin Chu. He gradually adapted to Yin Chu's casualness in dealing with her situation, her pompous attitude towards life, the absent-minded look and her tireless longing for sex. He perceived more mental factors in Yin Chu's aversion to hypocrisy, the motif of which was sex. For the first time, Luo Ke noticed something more intrinsic than looks through his intense and mirrored observation of ego without external actions. He saw a Luo-Keist. This was a man who was falling down in the flow of time. At every moment he experienced the chronic exhaustion of his heart, and sometimes he seemed to find a visionary ending. He knocked on the wall of life and listened to the empty echoes. He found himself lost in thought, immersed in the endless discussion of dual personality. He was an amnesiac who kept memorizing moral commandments, a fellow who personified organics, an ordinary player who was sent off the field by his dreams, and a man who equated a pause with meditation.

Luo Ke and Yin Chu saw each other as a friend in life and in spirit. They felt like they were keeping each other company on the guillotine of convention, at the same time looking for their Gods respectively like lovers after a tempest. They hoped to live in a miracle, which was the theoretical uniformity of feelings. Luo Ke realized that he was obsessed with everything transient. He thought one's attention to life could be boiled down to vacillating between others and oneself until one became dizzy and had to stop for a break.

The night air was chilly, with millions of stars hanging in the sky. A young man was fiddling with a motorcycle on the cement ground behind the apartment. He drove the motorcycle back and forth on the open ground, the exhaust pipes puttering like farting. The noise sounded impatient as if the muffler had been removed. A girl was talking with the motorcycle, twittering with a trill. The young man on the motorcycle did not speak from beginning to end.

Yin Chu was boiling the kettle to make tea in the kitchen, humming a tuneless melody while waiting for the water to boil. Luo Ke sat in the sofa cross-legged, facing the black-and-white TV with a big screen, lost in thought. The house was filled with the lingering smell of braised beef with potatoes after dinner. These days they were either in the room or in the movie theatre. They watched all the unbearable movies which were on—a man with blood pouring out of him looking up at the sky and making a deeply moving, long speech of his last words, a philosophical talk of a painful, solemn young man to a sorrowful girl in despair on a strange rock by the sea, a pair of unfeeling, slanted eyes (putting the theory of no-acting acting and low-profile acting into practice) staring at the camera for a long time with no reason, a length of disorganized fighting followed by a delicate love song, the prevalent, ubiquitous last-minute rescue, daily life performed in a high-class suite of a five-star hotel by assorted characters, the sentimental episode of a typical, immensely well-received bourgeois movie directed by a man of humble origin, unreasonable fighting of mafias (the cause was only enough for a slap), endless tears, endless laughter, boring and vulgar tragedies and extremely profound happy endings. In the meantime, they talked about all the aspects of their own life with certain reservation. Yin Chu commented after hearing part of Luo Ke's family history, "It seems to me that you'd rather be someone's son than be someone's father." Luo Ke retorted that it had to be so because he only had the experience of a son, not a father. Yin Chu sharply pointed out, "You are afraid of taking up the responsibility." Luo Ke defended himself again, "This is exactly being highly responsible." Every time their conversation proceeded to such a state as a court debate, Luo Ke would become unreasonable and started talking nonsense, giving a title of stinking bullshit to everything and everyone Yin Chu mentioned. For that Yin Chu called him the eastern envoy of the era of bullshit, but at the same time she shared her joy brought by his naive cries. "I know why Yin Mang liked you, though you have to understand that I'll leave you too." She did not explain why. She wanted him to know this, because he said that he was used to living in partings, keeping memories of the past and a little expectation of the future. "All these things only have an empty shell," Luo Ke explained. The relationship between them seemed to have reached a depth which could only be made possible by co-creation, but they might lose it at any time. He was either lost in the depth or floating on the surface. The life of a man like him was completely arranged by passion. He was constantly facing propositions of loyalty, betrayal or death. Of course there was another kind of people, whose life was regular and would only demonstrate some passionate signs in an extremely rare instant by careful arrangement. Such life was full of vitality, unlike that of Luo Ke, who only listened to the rhythm of his heart. Every day he needed to spend a long time on his flush toilet reading a book or discussing problems with others during a bowel movement. He remembered that in order to avoid the harmless gas he had released, Yin Mang had to stand on the edge of the bathtub and stuck her head out of the small square window of He Dafen's house to breathe fresh air. Meanwhile Luo Ke would discuss some theoretical problems with her. "You should read Saul Bellow's works. It was he who pointed out the so-called creativity of art, as far as its relationship with human souls was concerned, was great ridicule of the misery of man. He thinks that the creation of those talented lunatics is like digging underground tunnels, the ends of which will never meet with all their efforts. They lack necessary understanding of each other."

Yin Chu walked in up straight like a ballerina. Luo Ke looked at the cup in her hand and said, "I don't drink black tea. I don't like that smell." Yin Chu glanced at him and put the cup. "There's no green tea. How about boiled tap water? I drink that, too. You don't have much money but you are so picky." Yin Chu's preference for boiled tap water was something that she could not explain. What could not be explained either was her manner in which she gave others a lecture. The origin of these eccentricities was nowhere to be traced or verified just like the disappearance of some mysterious tribes. Perhaps Yin Chu thought she was born with the right to be haughty while other people (especially men) must bear her arrogance and rudeness. Luo Ke once made a profound speech about pride. He explained that most people lived in a small circle in which they respected each other. The circle included several friends, relatives (sometimes not including a wife) and rich and powerful men (his boss, for example). But out of this circle, he did not respect others any more. Only a few people make respecting others one of their basic principles, and you could generally call them big fools.

Of course, Yin Chu learned from Yin Mang a long time ago that Luo Ke was not someone you needed to treat too seriously. It was either his argument or his way of presenting that was not serious. At least one of them. Apart from hanging out with women, he did not have a so-called circle of his own. Wherever he went, he wanted to play the king, but he was always and would always be a glib jester. His cowardice and refinement were like twin brothers, which were so similar on the surface that others had no way to tell them apart and therefore equated one with the other.

No matter whom Luo Ke met, he would state his literary dream as routine. It was not to gain the honorable title as a cultivated artist, but purely based on a stubborn thought, "If others can do this, I can do this too." At such times, "others" usually referred to new writers who had just cut a figure like Sun Shu and Zhu Ke. Now he reviewed his personal writing history, looked into the future of the clamorous literary society in front of Yin Chu and finally concluded, "The so-called inspiration is that you suddenly think of something, but I will never suddenly come up with anything. How fortunate! My brain doesn't work well." The masterpiece that Luo Ke had repeatedly talked about and studied many times might eventually be dissolved by his theory of talking but not writing. It was as if the excitement brought by the slight traces of an early pregnancy were shaken to pieces by the bang of a rubber stamp which produced "negative" after a urinalysis.

"You'll ruin yourself by idling about like this," Yin Chu said to Luo Ke.

"You sound like my father. But don't you feel odd by saying such things? Aren't you living freely while ruining yourself?"

"Bullshit!" Yin Chu shouted at Luo Ke, "You don't deserve to have the tea I made for you. Get your ass off the couch and go draw your basins and spittoons. You think I'm a novel that you could just casually comment on? Put down the cup! You son of a bitch. You are a pig. You know that? You are a complete pig! A pig who loves talking about art!" Yin Chu was moved by her own hysteria. She sipped from her own cup, went to sit in another couch and started weeping, her tears streaming down her pale cheeks.

Luo Ke and Yin Chu sat still in separate couches. Yin Chu kept sobbing like a girl who was wronged, while Luo Ke stared at the cup of tea silently, just as a mole that had been busy digging holes suddenly got the time to take a rest and stared at the air at a loss.

17

Luo Ke walked home at night. He thought that taking a walk might rid himself of Yin Chu's crying, and therefore walked in circles on purpose, expecting the empty streets to ease his pain. The lovers in the shadow of the trees by the pavement were like characters in shadow puppetry, either remaining still or wriggling. Those postures were like kissing and to some extent like judo performance. Luo Ke came to find a truth in it. If one examined all the relationships a little, one would find a common sign—the couple was so intimate that they would fight each other. Both royalties and common people were no exception. As to the stormy romantic episodes of those famous people, what did Nabokov say? ("Most artists' private lives cannot stand a closer look.") In comparison, Luo Ke found that Yin Chu's shower of abuse was as transient as a sun shower during a walk in a Suzhou garden, which just served as a little seasoning. With such a self-massage and the night breeze brushing against his cheeks, Luo Ke thought he was lightened up and could go to sleep with a peaceful mind. But at the moment he had walked past the way to his house and therefore had to keep walking to finish the half circle left. As he regained calmness, the night view he had been neglecting reappeared in front of his eyes. Surrounded by the tall and long, fence-like, cement walls with a rough surface, a guard dog on a night patrol kept barking to demonstrate to its master that it was doing its job well. Next to the park was a Catholic church which had been deserted for a long time and was now under slow renovation. Its outer wall which had just been painted seemed fathomless in the moonlight. Ahead of it was the district library, a three-storied building standing by the street. The decorative pillars in front of it prevented its decrepitude from being completely concealed in darkness. Walking past a long row of newspaper board and the closed gate of the post office and fifty meters more, Luo Ke arrived at the door of the Big Strawberry Diner again. A young woman with heavy makeup stuck her body out of the door gap and looked around. She grinned on seeing Luo Ke. Despite her lovely appearance, her voice was flat when she started talking, "Eat?" She adequately withdrew her smile when she saw Luo Ke shaking his head. At that moment, the glass door was opened wider, and Zhu Ke's small head stuck out above the woman's head. "Luo Ke!" There was a hint of surprise in his voice, but afterwards he displayed his surprise in an unbridled manner. "What a surprise, Mr. Luo."

"What are you doing there?"

"Good question! What can I possibly be doing? Meeting friends and collecting material! Let me introduce her to you. This is Miss Shao." Zhu Ke patted her shoulder and appeared vigorous as if he were some special figure accustomed to night life.

The woman called Shao immediately pandered, "Invite your friend inside!" And she took a glance at Luo Ke.

"No," Luo Ke said weakly, "I'm going back to sleep. I'll come when I have time." He said against his wish and waved to Zhu Ke as saying goodbye. Luo Ke had barely taken a few steps when Zhu Ke caught up.

"Luo Ke, come inside. We haven't met for a long time. Let's have a chat." Zhu Ke suddenly turned sincere.

"Look at that woman. She runs a gang restaurant. Mind that she simmers you."

"Enough of that. You are not a girl. Why the cautiousness?" Zhu Ke said in a sarcastic tone to evening up his running after Luo Ke.

"Fine. If you have anything to say, just say it here." Luo Ke halted.

There was nothing dramatic in the acquaintance of Luo Ke and Zhu Ke. They were in the same high school, and Zhu Ke was one grade higher than Luo Ke. They were both substitutes in the school basketball team. Neither had played in a formal game. They just mixed themselves in a group of people and made several driving layups before the main players went on the field. They were sent to the school team in spring when school started. In the summer before the term ended when the team was going to participate in a district championship, the number of the players needed to be cut down and Luo Ke and Zhu Ke were thus kicked out of the team. They went to the stinking PE staff room and returned their sneakers and sport shirts, which put an end to their association on campus. Zhu Ke graduated one year earlier than Luo Ke and went into a factory manufacturing hygiene products for women (rumor had it that his first piece was written on a soft sheet of toilet paper). After several years, Zhu Ke suddenly devoted himself to all kinds of night schools. It was said that in less than five years, he graduated from more than a dozen schools and gained dozens of certificates on a warm spring day. According to Zhu Ke himself, he finished hundreds of assorted courses. In the sixth year, he shuttled between different kinds of night schools as a part-time teacher and lectured on basic principles of literary writing to men, women, the young and the elderly from all walks of life. Zhu Ke was not only a prolific genius in writing, but also a professional in cultivating new writers. Every ten days or a month, he would present his latest achievement on all occasions. Zhu Ke was always energetic and lively, talking eloquently in high spirits wherever he went. He was an optimist insulated from melancholy, a tough man who did not know worry.

"It's a little embarrassing to say it," Zhu Ke murmured.

"Don't be. Just say it. I'm tired."

"The thing is, a publisher in another province wants to publish a novella collection of mine, and I want to invite your father Mr. Luo to write a foreword to it." Zhu Ke quickly pointed out the key issue. It was then that Luo Ke realized the true intention of the phone call a week ago.

"Zhu Ke, aren't you playing him? He's a playwright. How would he understand your stuff?"

"Wait, don't rush. Or you can write it for me and then put your father's name on it. What do you think?"

"Let's do it this way." Luo Ke decided to get rid of the jerk right away, "You write it yourself. Write whatever you want, and I'll ask Luo Yizhi to sign his name. How about that?"

Zhu Ke, who was a clever guy, immediately detected the sarcasm behind Luo Ke's clear-cut words but still remained unfazed. "Fine. Since you will help me with this, I know what to do."

Zhu Ke and Luo Ke shook hands as if they meant it on the street at midnight. Then Zhu Ke watched Luo Ke walk away.

Zhu Ke had made a plan for himself a long time ago. Once Luo Yizhi's signature was at hand, he would peddle his novella collection compiled by himself to every publishing house. "Yes." Zhu Ke took a breath of the chilly night air. He recalled the lines of a Korean movie which was characterized by tears, "Sincerity can make stones blossom."

18

Luo Yizhi sat in the taxi headed for the hospital, his body leaning against the seat next to his wife with a dim look on her face. The falling rain from the sky formed a curtain with white vapor in front of the windshield, as if the car were closely following a watering cart and having a free wash. Luo Yizhi thought the panic had passed at the moment, and he seemed to have regained his confidence in his heart. He felt that many things entered his view again. He even saw the direction indicators on the instrument panel in front of the driver. The gravitation when the car turned made his body lean towards the other side of the seat. I won! He said to himself. He saw the people taking shelter from the rain and the tramcars passing by each other. The dense flow of people outside the window, which would normally disturb him, was now familiar and peaceful to him. The natural phenomenon easily transformed people back to men and women and made them move on the street as if with great strength. Those moving bodies did not represent vitality or indicate fatigue. They held their umbrellas as if suggesting that they remained neutral in spirit. Luo Yizhi recovered his thinking and observation. The streets he was familiar with and the advertisements that turned unfamiliar kept coming into his half-closed eyes. The booking number of the Northwest Airlines, a Toyota, a yellowish drink, a huge homemade television, a fur coat, plus a glimpse of some new medicine for treating coronary heart diseases. Again he was impressed by the sense of order formed by the competing combinations of commodities.

The taxi stopped at a crossroad. The driver let out a curse when waiting for the traffic light to change color. Luo Yizhi was relieved. He felt that he finally went back to the world he could narrowly manage to cope with. He smiled towards his wife who was as withered as him.

Luo Ke did not come to the hospital to replace his mother until nine o'clock at night.

"Sorry, dad. I just got home."

Luo Yizhi gently waved his hands and stopped him from explaining.

Every time Luo Ke smelled the pungent mixture of alcohol, ammonia and formalin, he would start feeling unwell. Luo Ke had a natural fear of hospital, and with the merciless doctors and frowning patients, he would become a softhearted, compassionate, ascetic, virtuous man whose legs kept trembling once he stepped into the hospital.

After Luo Ke came off work, he went to Yin Chu's house and spent a long time there. When he came back he saw the note his mother left on the gas stove in the kitchen. In that instant, Luo Ke realized for the first time his attachment to his father, and the tender feelings astonished him. He dimly thought that he was supposed to be a heartless, undutiful son who could turn his back on his own flesh and blood; apart from his instant wills, there was not the slightest compassion left in his body, and all the affective factors accumulated over years were all destroyed by sudden impulses which constantly overtook him. The indistinctive sounds of the outside world warmly appealed to and confirmed his inherent needs. The potential needs which he was unable to confirm by himself followed the lead of the outside world without reservation. Telephone rings which flipped his heart, an unexpected letter, a fragment of a book, a captivating rest of a melody, memories evoked by scenery, an encounter on the pavement, lasting expectation for a movie, perplexed and sweet attention evoked by witchcraft. These fleeting things would all break into his unprepared mind. When he was pondering, everything moving before his eyes was hideous. Though mundane days were endless, time would compress them into metal, tiny, delicate, shimmering and ready to be forged by memory, staying permanently in a place you knew but could not identify. Now, pain and menace of death were looming over his father. He felt his father's anxiety which was beyond words. He had no faith in medication or care, only praying at heart that the mechanism of life itself would present its unknown secret again and let a life continue to exist in its usual way. The value and necessity of that life only lay in that he was a father, a son's father. The son was Luo Ke, who was already extremely feeble.

Luo Yizhi fell asleep slowly, breathing steadily but looking fatigued. His grey hair spread loosely on the pillow. Luo Ke did not dare to look at his father too closely. He was afraid of looking down like this from the bottom of his heart. In his memory, he could not find such scenes. He never seemed to have gazed his father at his bedside like this. Luo Yizhi's heavy breaths sounded so strange to him that he forgot his duty.

A beautiful young nurse came in for inspection. Seeing that Luo Yizhi was sound asleep, she exchanged a look with Luo Ke and went outside. It was still raining. Outside the broad window was utter darkness, with sounds of leaves being battered by wind and rain. Luo Ke could not face the stillness alone. He stood up, went out of the ward and walked to the on-call room.

"I want to call my girlfriend. Is that OK?"

"Go ahead. The phone is over there." The young nurse pointed in a direction. "But don't be too long. I'm waiting for a call," she said and buried her head in a fashion magazine.

Luo Ke called Yin Chu and got through. The phone was picked up only after one ring. A deep male voice was transmitted here by the telephone wire, coming across the rainy night. "Hello?" Luo Ke hesitated, "Sorry, wrong number." He put down the phone and lifted it up again immediately. He redialed Yin Chu's number, and once the phone was picked up, he said, "I'd like to speak to Yin Chu." "This is her." Her voice sounded a little surprised. "I knew it was you. Where are you calling from?"

"I'm at the hospital. My father is ill. I was going to talk to you about this."

"Then talk. I'm free." A series of creaks came out of the phone, which sounded like she sat down on the chair. "Talk now. I'm listening," she said in a gentle voice, as if she could tell beforehand what Luo Ke was going to say.

"But I'm not sure whether I've made the final decision."

"You mean you'll tell me when you have decided."

"I've decided, but I'm not sure ..." Yin Chu interrupted Luo Ke and sighed over the phone.

"I can say for sure that you have never made any real decision. You are always hesitating, which you take as thinking it over. I bet you are not even sure whether you have made up your mind to have sex with me. Now you want to tell me that you love me, right?" She paused and continued speaking as Luo Ke did not reply, "Which hospital?"

Luo Ke told her.

"OK. Now I'll tell you my decision. First, I'm coming over now. Second, I'm in love with you too."

"Who's that man?" Luo Ke immediately asked.

"My guardian."

"What?" Luo Ke was confused.

"Policeman! Now he's walking outside. Be careful and don't forget who I am," she said and hung up the phone.

The nurse looked at Luo Ke smilingly, "Broke up?"

"Sort of," he said.

19

Luo Ke had to review his relationship with Yin Mang again on his own. He personally thought that the intimacy between them was proper. Though it was a little hasty at the beginning and a little absurd at the end, undoubtedly it was a brilliant spiritual glide. It swept the fake scape off the flower of love with pure affection, lifted it up from the ground in front of the storm of worldly views and made it rise up happily and blindly. Its invisible sublimation was like an act of relief towards failure, though it would eventually be blocked by the vast sea. At the same time, it symbolized the convergence of the waters of affection and a distant look in the depths of the heart. He saw clearly how the stream of affection flowed strangely along the watercourse of rationality.

She discussed with Luo Ke her relationship with Sun Shu with almost no disguise, pointing out everything absurd about it, but she knew that Sun Shu was the man that she ought to marry. "He's a husband, even if he's evil, not to mention that he's too kind. He has many faults, but he's a husband. Luo Ke, you are not." He still remembered the scene when Yin Mang announced this wise saying. With a sheen of maturity on her face, she purposefully used a childlike tone to pick her words, as if she were practicing spelling with a teacher dissolved in the air and accidentally uttered the harsh truth.

"I'm going to end the story between you and me." When she said that, she was choosing a suitcase with Luo Ke in front of a counter of a department store. "Please stop your feelings for me. Neither of us should disturb each other with things that have expired. If you don't listen to me, I'll have to fall in love with you again," she said the last sentence in an apparently joking tone.

Yin Mang did not belong to those who gradually rid themselves of childishness according to the golden law of nature. Her epic revolution of mind was accomplished overnight. On a morning or evening, which could not be pinpointed due to her poor memory, (judging from a noticeable ray of sunlight outside the window, she could not figure out whether she had just woken up or was going to sleep) she thought and immediately announced to herself that the historic event of remolding herself had been completed. Yin Mang shared with Luo Ke her recollections—she suddenly realized the essence of the world, which scared her. Yin Mang took out her pen and the exquisite diary book preferred by girls on the spot and made a statistical, true and meticulous record of the eve of the revolution. Part of the material of her documentary literature was as follows: The night before she ate a large plate of braised chicken when having dinner with her classmates; she finished reading the explicit autobiography of Isadora Duncan; the pocket money sent by her mother was tragically cut down by half for the first time; she got all the questions about the frigging function words wrong in a test of ancient Chinese prose; for the first time someone described her as plump in an anonymous love letter; the incessant menstrual floods which she extremely detested and yet bore with equanimity; for the first and also the last time she was inebriated, (By whom? She asked herself), followed by raving, crying, vomiting, headaches and embarrassment. Also, she improvised, "I'll meet you and fall in love with you." Such sensitive, perceptive insight into the future was assembled by her unnoticeable sophistication and unaffected artlessness, though Yin Mang was indeed a young woman used to disguising herself. She would present a performance of making herself up from time to time and was deeply moved to see herself away from the worldly hubbub.

As to Luo Ke, he was merely marking time with the same rhythm as that of Yin Mang. It was just that Luo Ke lifted the left foot first while Yin Mang lifted her right foot (a funny and disordered parade drill).

Luo Ke, who was kind-hearted, fired a shot of slander with the gun of memory towards Yin Mang, who was walking out of his sight. The one brought down would be Yin Mang's substitute that was moving in front of the iron sight of jealousy—Yin Chu, who was far better.

20

Luo Ke dreamed of an elephant swatting a mosquito with its swinging trunk and stomping with rage. Then he woke up. A peal of ferocious cries of peddling came from outside the window. It seemed to be a man who recycled old clothes and radios in the neighborhood. Judging by the voice only, he could be taken as a member of a robber gang breaking into people's houses. Luo Ke felt that he was left behind the times. Overnight even those who ran small businesses improved their conditions, which conformed to the old saying, "He who has wealth speaks louder than others." Luo Ke reached out and turned on the radio on the desk. He turned it up to a deafening volume and curled back in his quilt. A husky voice was lamenting the impermanence of love. The tune was melodious but the male singer just mumbled the lyrics sloppily. Luo Ke did not know whether it was because he had not woken up or the singer mumbled the words on purpose. He waited for the singer to jolt him. After the husky voice slowly sang for a while, it suddenly turned to a sobbing tone. His voice became flat. The hissing sound reminded Luo Ke of the Gillette razor with a shiny blade. After sobbing for a while he started crying out, something to the effect that "If you don't love me, I might as well die." As far as the expressiveness of his husky voice was concerned, such exaggerated words lacked convincing infectiousness, though he repeated nearly ten times without a break no matter you were convinced it or not. When the song ended, he sighed with helplessness, as if saying, "Since you don't believe me, I'll stop singing."

The radio station seemed to be set against Luo Ke on purpose. Following the husky singing was the sweet voice of a hostess. She talked about the historical changes of rock music longwindedly in an affected pedantic manner, during which she dropped the names of several prominent figures in fluent pidgin English which was neither English nor Chinese translation (something like Springsteen). The sweet lady chattered endlessly with a lilting cadence. Luo Ke, bleary-eyed and compelled by the hypnosis of the broadcast, unknowingly fell into a light sleep again. The well-trained voice of the hostess metamorphosed into Yin Chu's flat, husky voice, pale and sexy. Following the proper nouns like Blues, Jazz Blues and Ragtime, a black young man's face emerged with sorrow and grace—Wright. Last night was a gloomy night with frequent urination, as Yin Chu's new foamy beer and her stories made Luo Ke's bladder as full as his head. The bubbles of beer irrigated his stomach but contaminated Yin Chu's flush toilet. As Yin Chu's new lover and listener, every time he felt that the two important parts of his body were pushed to the limit, he would go to the bathroom with a decent toe-out gait in slow haste. Watching one tank of water after another vie with each other to embrace his urine and take it into a deep hole, he was temporarily relieved by a sense that a great burden had been taken off him. The whole night was divided into several chapters by Luo Ke's excretions, and Yin Chu's Maslova-style stories were the dolorous content distributed among them.

In the prelude of the earthly comedy which involved two third-world countries and eventually sent the young and self-assertive Yin Chu to prison, Wright the hero was a noble son of the upper class of Zembla and a studious international student majoring in Japanese Yamaha motorcycle at some medical university (Yin Chu's sincere Wright had never disclosed any details). With a mixed smell of perfume and body odor, he was making sexy moves on the disco dance floor in a ballroom for athletes, as if inadvertently showing his brilliant butt moves to Yin Chu, who was madly bouncing on the spring floor. In the dazzling and colorful lighting, the silly girl Yin Chu happily and sweatily danced with the descendent of the father of disco. (No one could know for sure which genre Wright's dancing belonged to, as in the epilogue of "Yin Chu and Wright," a relevant party concluded in a thorough and discreet survey that his claim to have mastered the basics of acupuncture anesthesia was completely fabricated. Zembla was also sheer fiction. Wright the motorcyclist proved to have been a homeless man of unidentified nationality on a merchant ship made in the Netherlands, owned by West Germany and leased to Japan with French shareholders and an American captain.)

A dance ended, Wright ("Who on earth is he?" Yin Chu asked Luo Ke with red eyes.) had become a dancing partner who had developed mutual affection and tacit understanding with Yin Chu. He made no attempt to conceal his strong intention to develop their partnership in more extensive fields.

With his sweaty hands he dragged Yin Chu to the bar upstairs and started chatting with her with the typical humility of a drunkard before going on a binge. Among the five official working languages of the United Nations they chose English, which both of them could at least speak a little. "Whisky!" Wright shouted at the waiter. Yin Chu attended to Wright's English gingerly and asked him to repeat what he said from time to time in embarrassment. (Perhaps Wright's English was mixed with the accent of Zembla.)

Between the ballroom at night and the hotel room at night was a prompting series of telephone intermezzos. The black man Wright expressed his endless African affection as burning as the open country on the equator. In the continuous phone calls, he used a group of love phrases that Yin Chu had long been familiar with since their long talk at the bar. Yin Chu, with her heart growing amorous, felt unquenchably thirsty as if she were hit by tear gas.

Next Yin Chu was held up like a defendant on several details which Luo Ke refused to let go. Exhausted physically and mentally, she had to dissect her sex with Wright again and again, which was a round of intensive farming in the field of sensation, psychology and the depths of consciousness like a carpet bombing (Ah, Vietnam!). What a beautiful piece of virgin land! Luo Ke, with the stubbornness of an OCD patient, constructed the erotic picture sorrowfully in his mind based on the fragmented description. This picture, as if viewed through the peep hole of a kaleidoscope, was only relevant to Luo Ke's own experience. Yin Chu was only a part of the picture.

The ending of "Yin Chu and Wright" was that Yin Chu served two years in prison. In her brown handbag a roll of foreign currencies was found, but she could not explain the source of the all-powerful yet abominable money. Yin Chu's precious virgin blood was still on the white bed sheet in the hotel suite, but what happened to the blood-thirsty sword?

"I don't know!" Yin Chu suddenly shouted in Luo Ke's face.

"You should."

"I don't want to, you pig!"

21

The autumn air which freshened one's mouth and nose withdrew with an incessant drizzle from the streets and allies of this port city irreversibly. Pigeons with colorful feathers raised by individuals flew freely in the warm sky in early winter. They perched on the roofs and windowsills of other houses in groups and examined the world with the little red eyes on the two sides of their head, casually leaving behind disgusting smudges of feces. They flew without the pleasant and cheerful sound of pigeon whistles or simply forgot about that and became a species which only stayed in their dovecotes and ate more than they exercised. They were always considered the symbol of peace and felicity, but in the place where Luo Ke lived, they were synonymous with environmental pollution and neighbor dispute.

Apart from lecturing a group of diehard amateur opera fans, Luo Ke's upstairs neighbor, the famous tenor, set up a dovecote with a frame made of aluminum alloy on the balcony out of his disdain for popular music. Every morning, he sang out the lament of some foreigners over fate one or two centuries ago in Spanish, indirectly expressing his own lament over the irony of life in the face of these angelic pets. "For art, for love." The tenor glanced at his wife who was making the bed, "Alas!" He sang the recitative, "Forget it! Forget it!" And the "artist's business" of the day ended.

Luo Ke had long been used to the etude which always started well but ended sloppily. He hid in the room, poured water for himself and gave himself a cigarette to smoke, quietly thinking about the past. He stood by the dusty windowsill and looked outside with concentration, trying his best to eliminate the distractions both in the outside world and in his heart. It was not long before he gave up the yoga plan in frustration. He realized in despair that he was no longer able to meditate on his own with the stir of life. He had lost patience with his personal life which was filled with confusion, deficiency and tension, as well as the dazzling kaleidoscopic world which made one lose one's sense. As far as Luo Ke was concerned, living alone meant looking back to the past and feeling deep regret with idiotic detachment towards everything at the same time. With his mind growing increasingly rigid, he felt the need to immerse himself in the conversation with anyone but he was also afraid of others' words which were sometimes almost incomprehensible. He never thought of himself as a worrier. He knew that sometimes he would exaggerate the pain and distort it to gain an eccentric sort of comfort. But living like a parasite for some time would always bring about a veil of depression and cause Luo Ke to be steeped in worry accompanied by boredom. On the surface he was happy in every moment but these naughty moments combined would lead to a depressing day and a night spent on boring conversations and drinking down sorrow. At certain moment he firmly believed that his unfortunate state was not appropriate but immediately he would come up with a contrary thought and find some appropriateness in the inappropriateness to console himself. Such self-sufficiency in comfort usually involved abstracting philosophical notions from daily life after elevating all of it indiscriminately to a universal level and then giving them back to oneself in plain language with a common touch. The idea of reclusion started occurring to him from time to time, but he could not pick out an ideal place to live in solitude, not to mention that a phone call or a scribbled letter could summon him back to the life he was fed up with a minute ago. Under these circumstances Luo Ke usually excluded Yin Chu from his thoughts, as that was counterproductive to the original aim of thinking wildly. It was precisely the pain of love that made him play the role of a thinker. Philosophy was pure, which was just enough to allow Luo Ke to get rid of his artistic bitterness.

At the moment, three meters above Luo Ke's head filled with random thoughts was a half-retired middle-aged man sitting silently and bitterly in front of his beloved object and old fellow—a brand new Hero piano. He lifted the lid and took a look inside, the fragrance of mothballs wafted from the tightened steel wire and organized hammers. The keys were closely-connected and the pedals screaked when pressed down. The happiness and satisfaction which he had been expecting most of his life clearly came at an inappropriate time. The chorus he was in was suddenly kicked off the stage like an unfortunate star by those singers who ran all over it while singing. He had stood on the wobbly wooden bench for decades, complementing the first tenor and the soprano whose voices shot for the sky with his bright and gentle voice as the second tenor, touring the rivers in Russia and the Alps. He also depicted the great Anti-Japanese War and the unprecedented Great Leap Forward in detail with his fellow on the bench. He clearly remembered the sense of fellowship which permeated the different parts of their choir as if they were siblings during the acappella performance. He also remembered the sense of achievement when he first held the program list on which the words "Leading singer: Gao Ge" were printed.

The middle-aged man whose stage name was Gao Ge pressed the F-sharp in the two-lined octave and listened to his humming while covering one of his ears with the left hand. Below the back key his voice was as gentle as the soulful singing of a mezzo-soprano, but it would unconsciously turn metallic once the note was higher than the black key. (But it was the alloy-with-rusty-spots-and-tightened-vocal-cords kind of metallic voice.) Gao Ge's epencephalon was well developed, perhaps because of the influence of his singing. Though he was an ingenuous man who never stabbed others in the back, he would still shout curses at his wife with his clear and sonorous voice at the speed of a march which could shake the house.

His clamorous daughters twittered all day long like a children's chorus full of vitality. Their silvery shouting and bawling was led by his high-pitched voice, as if they were performing a modern piece with jarring Bartokish harmony and novel techniques.

The chorus included an angry father, his elated daughters, their mother wearing a long face and a bunch of pigeons they raised. What little common knowledge Luo Ke had about chorus came from that.

22

Yin Mang's family (including Yin Chu, whom Luo Ke knew relatively well, as well as other miscellaneous members he was less acquainted with) had been living for nearly half a century in the Xicun Apartment, which was designed by and constructed under the supervision of a British man named John Wilson in 1939. At the beginning it was Yin Dongshan's girlfriend back in his school days that helped him rent an apartment in it. (What a sweet moment fifty years ago!) After a long, boisterous and ignorant premarital etude of love, Yin Dongshan, standing at the thick and smooth teakwood door, received three wives of different styles successively into his house. Though the talented railway engineer was a man with special interests in marital life, such unmentionable personal foibles did not affect his lofty image as a precious patriot. His unparalleled wisdom in the field which he devoted his life to far exceeded the intelligence of his thirteen children in total, who lacked dedication towards their work but excelled in certain other areas. The father secretly passed on his unique understanding of life and strong interest in the past to his children, like an acknowledged gardener who transformed his personal greenhouse into the House of Green Delights filled with beautiful flowers. His pigheaded children all had their own way and had already messed up in every corner of the world even before their father died, leaving Yin Dongshan dumbfounded. There was enough said earlier about Yin Chu who was a household name in the society page of the evening paper. Yin Mang, his good girl, was involved in the love triangle with Luo Ke and Sun Shu before graduation. His seventh son, the prodigy who devoted himself to music in compensation of his father's tone-deafness, was prohibited from leaving the country by law as he was a suspect in smuggling and reselling cultural relics after securing a letter of recommendation signed by Professor Gontier himself at the French Conservatory of Music. His eldest son was bogged down in the prolonged divorce proceedings just like him. His other children either went to the frontier in a special period to share the destiny with their country or went to live with their grandparents after they endured the special period together with their mother. Yin Dongshan was not a model of sacrificing family for justice, but he was indeed a scatterbrained blunderer. Perhaps because he was incapable of caring for such a big family, he had to take a laissez-faire approach, which eventually led to his unspeakable sorrow and misery. After his death and Yin Mang's going abroad, his third wife (Yin Mang's mother) left the Xicun Apartment and moved back to the old house at *shikumen* where she lived with her parents before marriage. Then came the juncture at which their family started falling apart. An unidentified man, who claimed to be some woman's son, came to reclaim the house with a wrinkled contract signed fifty years ago. The man filed his pleading, causing Yin Dongshan's eldest son to run between two courts. At that time Yin Chu was instructed to guard their so-called home, the desolate house in imminent peril.

Judging from Yin Chu's relationship with Wright, which was condemned by the public, she was not a racist. There was no trace of South African racism against black people in her; she might have even considered marrying him. The minor setback in her life affected certain aspects like the way she treated people. She was no longer concerned about men's largely similar sweet words and developed an exclusive trick in dealing with platitudes in the form of a lover's whisper, which was staring at the private parts of the speaker with a cold expression as if she were evaluating the tailor's skill. Once a dumb ass stated that he saw "wordless poetry" in her downcast eyes, which made her laugh for literally a whole afternoon. Yin Chu was an expert in this respect. She was good at identifying a playboy based on unnoticeable signs, and would instinctively set up a line of defense once she met one, turning women's reserved manner into laughing and cursing. In Luo Ke's eyes, Yin Chu was not gorgeous; nor was she one of those unwary yet unapproachable women. She, with bright eyes and droopy mouth corners, was a housekeeping master who specialized in disciplining her husband. Yin Chu valued family, like her half-sister Yin Mang. Her highest criterion for men was "husband."

But sometimes, there would occur something unexpected but reasonable in life for the sake of its structure, like those in novels. For example, when Luo Ke called on a rainy night and faltered over the phone while she was sitting next to a conscientious officer, she would allow her principles to take a break, follow the surging waves of her will, and reply with some long-prepared words of love with only a few adaptations.

People would often develop a harmless illusion about their busy life. After she was given parole, Yin Chu always took it that she was trying to start a new life according to some amended rules which people were willing to accept. It was related to her first sleepless night in prison. She had thought that she would be able to fall asleep quickly without any concern due to her mental exhaustion, but in fact she did not know what to do other than move her stare on the cold wall. Her mean-looking, combative inmate was a good snorer who produced successive loud snores as if testifying to her disturbed mind, causing Yin Chu to have nightmares with her eyes open. She saw a wild beast that she had never seen. It was neither a tiger nor a leopard. Following a beam of moonlight that leaked into the cell, it dived into her body, hanging around among her viscera. The nameless creature with colorful fur made sounds of different pitches from time to time, as if talking. She was especially surprised that she should understand what it meant. It was a warning foreboding the hemorrhage which made her pass out the next dawn. After that fantastic night, Yin Chu believed that she could hear the conversation between her internal organs before any pathological change took place, as if they were tipping her off. She bribed them with newly-developed sugarcoated pills or a hot-water bag. If they happened to be in a good mood and put behind the instigation of the beast for the moment, they would spare her the pain. Yin Chu viewed her submission to the beast as her submission to life. She educated herself on the effects of smoking by reading some popular scientific articles, and scared herself with the risks of insobriety. Keeping a tight rein on her behavior brought comfort to her rationality, which lightened her up and made her agile. While for the first time happiness came to her in a healthy way, assorted desires managed to make a comeback. Ruled again by her desires, Yin Chu sank into a new round of battle between her body and soul. With a deep understanding of being, she said to herself, "Let your body win first, and then let your soul get the better of it."

At the beginning, Yin Chu and Luo Ke learnt the subtleties of their affection through poker and chess games. They complimented on each other's poor chess skills, mercilessly captured the pawns which reached their side, constantly asked to retract a move, and slayed all of the other's pieces once they had the chance. They spent more time playing poker. Every time they would start with some extremely simple games and soon entered a relatively complex stage of probing into fate. Telling fortune through playing cards was the most will-sapping game that made one's senses sharp and one's mind fuzzy. It adequately united their lethargy by turning them into an excuse for each other's inertia.

The distance between the desk for playing games and the bed of significance was long. When they were both calm, it seemed unlikely in the foreseeable future. They blocked each other from the outside world. Sometimes they would inquire of some acquaintances about what happened in the city which was like a big village, only to be disturbed by the hearsay and lose their hard-cultivated gentle mood. Many fine moments were disrupted by teasing. On a listless evening, Yin Chu came across a romantic piece of work on a magazine when waiting for the routine harassment of the owner of the house. She recommended the verse to Luo Ke, who was dozing, and let him appreciate the fine poem which praised women's body. Luo Ke rubbed his slightly sore eyes and replied with reluctance, "What's the big deal? According to the dictionary, *dong* of the word *dong ti* (body) refers to intestines, and *ti* refers to torso. Do you know what a torso is? Let me tell you, it's the body without the head, limbs and guts." "Bullshit!" Yin Chu objected. "Probably." Luo Ke stretched his body on the sofa and continued to comment, "It's dangerous to praise *dong ti*, which carries a sexual hint. Better praise the soul, like what you and I have been doing." Luo Ke closed his eyes again and curled up. He snickered, "So what I've heard about praising the soul is to make it fall asleep? Wait, according to the dictionary, it's the body that falls asleep."

23

It was nine o'clock at night. Yin Chu was lying on the bed prone like a soldier, with a shiny silver pin on her belt buckle. She was thinking about Wright, the liar. The son of the deceased Yin Dongshan's girlfriend fifty years ago was standing in the doorway with a self-assured air of the property owner.

"Excuse me, is Yin Chu at home? I've come by appointment."

"You are late," Luo Ke said.

"I'm Qiao Guangzhong." He raised his arm and flashed the ring on his finger, stroking his hair with the arrogance of a son from a rich family. "Who are you?"

"I'm Yin Chu's lawyer." Luo Ke was quick and articulate, which surprised Qiao Guangzhong, who was wearing a well-ironed suit. He tucked his chin a little and glanced at Luo Ke's hair that stuck out with his bulging eyes behind the gold-rimmed glasses.

"I made an appointment with Yin Chu. How can she not show up?"

"You are late. She went out on an errand."

"What could she possibly have to deal with?" Qiao Guangzhong mumbled, as if knowing everything about Yin's family.

"You want to talk with me or come another day?"

"I'm fine with both." The unconfirmed owner of the house threw the potato back to Luo Ke.

"The thing is, if you talk with me, you'll be wasting your time because I don't call the shots here. If you come another day, you'll have to make another appointment with Yin Chu. It's up to you," Luo Ke said.

Qiao Guangzhong, a sophisticated, tactful man who would haggle over trifles, immediately saw through the evil intention of the fake lawyer. He neither left nor came inside on his own without being invited. He positioned himself in front of the door and started making noises in the corridor. He wanted to create a topic of conversation among the neighbors and lay the social foundation for his entering the Xicun Apartment one day. He made lengthy speeches in the empty corridor, starting from historical development, in which he particularly stated the eternal morals and improving laws that every citizen (the Yins in particular) should obey as the justice system was growing mature. In the meanwhile he emphasized the miserable outcome of disdaining social norms by asking questions and then answering them by himself. Qiao Guangzhong knew that those warm-hearted neighbors were enjoying his speech, pressing their ears against the door. He continued his emotional, half-true speech based on his knowledge of the loyal audience he had never met as an experienced broadcaster.

Luo Ke leaned against the door, arms crossed, listening to the speech of the corridor parrot with a weary, indifferent and concentrated look of a recordist. Qiao Guangzhong was good at what he was doing. He appealed to the potential audience with a rhythmic flow of preaching instead of desperate shouting. You could see the face of a helpless man, which suddenly turned into the innocent face of a humiliated yet benevolent man who was asking his audience for justice. He did not care how the fake lawyer Luo Ke would react, as if the only aim of his visit was to preach in the corridor.

Luo Ke thought he would find Qiao Guangzhong's lengthy speech a nuisance, but the short distance between them made him feel like a linesman, who was neither like the panting player running all over the field nor the fanatic audience who shouted like crazy but did not help at all. He was not the referee, either, who could send somebody off the field so long as he felt like showing a red card. He was someone both relevant and irrelevant to the game. He was someone in between, who ran back and forth along the sideline, constantly waving the flag in his hand. In theory he should be unfeeling because it was his flag that disintegrated one exciting attack after another. Yes, offside. That was how Luo Ke viewed the stories of fighting when one crossed the line. Those guys who were faster than others eventually found themselves in an area they were not yet supposed to be.

Qiao Guangzhong was at first stirred by his own words, but then gradually lost his enthusiasm. Facing Luo Ke who appeared asleep, he was disheartened. He felt like a fool trapped in the web spun by himself and disturbed by his own noises. He did not know when to stop or whether he should continue and break the cocoon of words in the end to fly around silently like a moth, putting an end to the journey started by wriggling and nibbling.

Luo Ke did not remember what Qiao Guangzhong said before he left in a huff. He said to himself, "You should wake up and check on your lover who was fixed on the bed by a silver pin."

There was no sound at all. Luo Ke thought Yin Chu might have fallen asleep. He walked into the west-facing room and saw Yin Chu sitting on the bed upright, legs crossed, gulping down water from the glass in her hand. She lifted her head, "You should at least make some noise. I thought you left with that stand-up comedian."

"That's impossible."

"Why?"

"I almost fell asleep."

"What do you think of him? Is he well-dressed, eloquent and gentlemanlike?"

"Exactly."

"Do you know what he does? You have no idea. He's the lift operator in the district hospital. The kind of lift in our building. He helped transport the dead into the morgue."

"It's true that life toughens people. All the vigor he had in the corridor turns out to be developed by facing the freshly dead bodies."

Volume III

1

Luo Ke's mother was an agile, plump old lady. Someday she might be described as a folk heroine who was proficient in *qigong*, medicine, swordsmanship and mind reading. She was an active participant in assorted leisure-time activities. As she was overshadowed by her playwright husband for years, her extraordinary talent in making mundane things brilliant receded in terms of its scope of influence. She was good at making up all sorts of gossip in the congenial atmosphere when visiting relatives and friends. She was devoted to such highly competitive mental activities. As far as the stirring effect was concerned, her storytelling skills were unparalleled compared with the chattering housewives. But she never prided herself on it; nor did she boast in front of her erratic son, let alone competing with her accomplished husband. She was a humble, good-tempered wife and mother who knew when to exert pressure, believed in compromise, and would spare no effort to mediate when necessary.

Luo Ke's mother got up at dawn every day and went to the nearby small park to practice her feeble sword dancing which combined the merits of all styles. There was not the slightest sense of malevolence which belonged to the villains in kungfu movies on the edge of her sword. The slowness of its motion suggested that it could not even cut open the air. After the warm-up, she walked in measured steps along the winding cement path in the park. On the way she would observe different schools of kungfu of men and women of different ages. While there were indeed some masters with consummate skills hidden in the trees, there were more laymen in garish clothes demonstrating their inferior techniques with sounds like "Ha!" to attract others' attention. Luo Ke's mother kindly smiled on all of this. She well understood the meaning of such scenes in the park. The naughty children today would become the elderly tomorrow, and the vitality of the park in the morning sunshine brushed away the sorrow and labor of yesterday—these were what those ruddy martial arts practitioners who knew how to preserve their health would rather not mention.

It was in this small park steeped in the beauty of late autumn that Luo Ke's mother ran into Yin Chu's neighbor, Luo Ke's biology teacher in middle school. Luo Ke's mother vaguely remembered that she seemed to have met the grinning man once on a parent-teacher meeting, which immediately helped her recognize the man with loose features and sallow skin. Inhaling and exhaling the fresh air, Mr. Gao radiated with vigor. They said good morning to each other and started inquiring after each other. They complimented on each other's complexion and wished each other longevity. Then their topic was changed as Mr. Gao worriedly recounted Luo Ke and Yin Chu's love story with some help of imagination. At last he concluded with the authority of an insider that her good son was falling into an abyss. When her face suddenly changed color and appeared to be disturbed, Mr. Gao stopped talking in a timely manner and walked away with a leisurely gait of a visitor as if nothing had happened.

Flying into a rage was not the specialty of Luo Ke's mother. As an expert in women's problems, she knew how much truth there was in the gossip from a man. But her motherly instinct made her decide that she should talk with her son. She did not count on that to make her son change his mind. She just wanted to exert a little influence or detect in Luo Ke's equivocation even the slightest sign to relieve her anxiety.

Her attempt, which sparked fury from Luo Ke, was instantly

dashed. He smashed the teacup in his hand on the spot and stormed towards the Xicun Apartment with the rage of an avenger who lost his head.

As a usual result of Luo Ke's resolution, his revenge plan existed in name only when he was just half way there. In his mind he had knocked down the womanish faggot a hundred times. When he took the first step on the staircase in the pitch-dark apartment building, his mind was occupied with the thought of crying out loud in Yin Chu's arms. "Men's foibles." Yin Mang once commented on such vulnerability which came out of nowhere.

2

Timid as Luo Ke was, he had a strong desire to confide in others. Though normally he would evaluate the situation so as not to pick the wrong listener, he could still make mistakes sometimes as a man who remained true to his feelings.

Luo Ke roamed the streets for a long time in the afternoon and bought two volumes of foreign comic books which included Yin Chu's favorite works. She once read the comics in a magazine about a housewife who hid books in the refrigerator among others. After that he waited in a queue of four or five people in front of a delicatessen and bought 500 grams of rabbit meat which was also Yin Chu's favorite. Luo Ke put everything in a plastic bag and, thinking that Yin Chu's habit of eating snacks might never change, felt as if he were tinted with Lily Hellman's sweet melancholia.

When Yin Chu came to open the door for Luo Ke in a brand new casual sport suit and slippers, his great revenge plan was brushed aside by his little everyday joy.

There was someone else in the room.

"Ou Xiaolin," Yin Chu introduced her to Luo Ke.

"So you are Luo Ke!" Ou Xiaolin rose up from the couch

and gave him a firm handshake. She was wearing the same pink casual sport suit as Yin Mang, hair pulled back in a thick and short ponytail. She seemed full of youthful vigor, as if beneath her fair skin there were a red light which made her face glow.

"Isn't it beautiful?" Yin Chu could not wait to show Luo Ke her new sport suit, which was given to her by Ou Xiaolin. Luo Ke had heard from Yin Chu that Ou Xiaolin was a famous theater academy student who had always played someone's mischievous sister in several feature movies. Yin Chu used a brilliant example in illustrating that the actress was a character—"She never wears a bra." The phrase Ou Xiaolin most frequently used was "screw up." She said that she screwed up her school years and reputation, screwed up all the movies she was in and all the male directors of those movies, and at the same time those incapable directors also screwed her up.

Perhaps the only thing Ou Xiaolin would not "screw up" was her friendship with Yin Chu, probably because all the trials she experienced made her sympathetic to what Yin Chu had went through. Once or twice a year, she would come back from filming locations which allegedly included places like Urumchi or Lhasa, and despite her toil, she would talk all night long with Yin Chu, sobbing curses on men.

Ou Xiaolin used to be Yin Mang's friend. On a night five or six years ago, she retreated from a less well-known director's house and dragged all her luggage like a soldier carrying impedimenta to Yin Mang's to spend the night. It happened that Yin Mang was out. Yin Chu and she talked with each other as if they had been old friends. It was a night of confidence. Since then Ou Xiaolin became Yin Chu's confidant and drifted away from Yin Mang, with whom she only made small talks over the phone.

Yin Chu pulled a low round table over and took out a bottle of domestic whisky brought by Ou Xiaolin. She poured the movie star a drink, herself a glass of boiled water, and Luo Ke a glass of beer. The three of them skipped the toast and clinked their glasses in silence. Each took a sip and sat down on a couch, an armchair and a cane chair respectively. Yin Mang, their common acquaintance, naturally became the subject of their conversation. They predicted Yin Mang's odds of survival in Australia based on hearsay, scenery footages on TV and descriptions in newspapers and magazines, in both optimistic and pessimistic ways. Surprised at their indifferent tone, they changed the subject. They listened to Ou Xiaolin brag about a war movie she was shooting, about how she was commissioned by Generalissimo Chiang to assassinate a secret agent with double identity played by a famous actor in a mystifying movie named *Assassination Order*. She vividly described how she swiftly pulled her gun and shot a repulsive extra who came at her while screaming in a decrepit stinky warehouse. She showed Luo Ke and Yin Chu how the whimsical director asked her to shoot a supporting actor with an impossible wrist posture and shooting angle in front of the camera. She patted her right hip and said, "I'm gonna be disabled." The cause was her falling from a horse a week ago. "It's the first time I put on a plaster. I just can't stand the smell of it. I don't even know how to describe it," she added. At last she concluded with one sentence, "The movie was screwed up." When Yin Chu asked who was responsible, Ou Xiaolin replied with an authoritative tone, "Nobody on our team has used a gun before. It's only weird if it's not screwed up." "Not necessarily." Yin Chu said, "They can just hire a military advisor." "A military advisor?" Ou Xiaolin laughed heartily, "What do they need him for? They even want to replace the horses with mules."

Luo Ke was infected by Ou Xiaolin's lively description. With successive glasses of beer, he felt that such a conversation full of gestures was great fun. He rose from the chair and mimed the play he watched on TV in front of the two ladies, which kept himself rolling about. When he realized that the two ladies were not laughing and that they were merely looking at him gently, he had to sit back in his chair and then immediately rose up and went to the toilet. When he got back after relieving himself in the toilet, Ou Xiaolin made it a point to add a comment, "Your TV is screwed up in your hands."

"Do you plan to be a movie actress forever?" Luo Ke asked.

"Why should I plan? As if a lifetime were a long time. What do you think, Yin Chu?" Ou Xiaolin rested her legs on the edge of the couch.

"Your legs are still so beautiful." Yin Chu did not answer her question.

"Nonsense. I already screwed them up. I don't even dare to go swimming in summer or stride on the street in a dress. I don't have any role to play other than a female spy of the Bureau of Investigation and Statistics, who always wears breeches," Ou Xiaolin commented on herself as if elated.

Ou Xiaolin was an attractive traveler as dazzling as a butterfly. She was also upbeat and forgetful. Her departures and arrivals were always accompanied by an earth-shattering tumult, as if a mob swarmed into a granary. She often left such private belongings as her leather trunk with wheels and denim travel bag with someone, as if they were left by a deceased explorer, and then disappeared like a wanderer who went into the depths of a desert with no word ever heard from her. After a year or so, she would come back, with a solemn look as if she had survived great perils, to her mundane life as a normal person. Normally at that time she would be with a new trunk and a new travel bag. Luo Ke secretly concluded that the peculiarity of such wanderers as indulged in a life of horse riding like Ou Xiaolin was not their travel-stained life, but rather the almost inhumanly intense exercise of the body that spared her the mental state of suspended animation. Luo Ke deemed that everyone would at least experience one period of mental shock in their life, and in such a secluded state of self-imprisonment, one would come back to the dreamy surface of one's secular life. In such periods, one's spirit would degenerate from the highest level of summoning to the lowest level of imploration. One's life would be defined as erotic and lonely. Ou Xiaolin moved here and there like a rabbit, relying on the rapidly changing views and focuses to avoid the sweet empty state referred to as mental shock by Luo Ke.

As far as Ou Xiaolin herself was concerned, what distinguished her from others (Luo Ke, for example), was that both her emotions and her way of expressing them were simple and straightforward. And for that matter, Yin Chu was her ally. Though Luo Ke shared the same quality in his emotions, he expressed them while trying to trace their origin and evaluating their nature, which left him lost in a transparent state of entanglement. Luo Ke was an immortal loser, whose imperishable achievement was making one mistake after another. His inevitable final image was a virtuous slave, though he could not safely reach that destination yet. He was a man who kept hovering on his journey, a wolf in the wildness, an isolated exile who tried to save his soul through warfare.

The amber whisky flowed through Ou Xiaolin's body from her throat, and the physical and mental satisfaction blurred her vision. She felt as if someone were knotting her tongue. She continued talking, trying to be articulate with great effort. She deduced from the listless look of Luo Ke and Yin Chu that they were used to their unexciting life and pronounced that they would enter a stage characterized by despair and inertia.

"Comrade Luo, you seem to be closely tied with the Yins, but I'm certain that leading this kind of life like a fly flying aimlessly around will destroy you. Do you believe it?"

"Then what do you suggest I do?" Luo Ke asked.

"Two options. Either you leave this place and go back to live with your parents and find a girl to marry and have children or ... What did I say? Yin Chu, tell him how many options I've mentioned."

After nearly a bottle of whisky, Ou Xiaolin fell asleep.

"She's exhausted." Yin Chu raised her head, looking at Luo Ke, "She's quite beautiful, right?"

"She is, and also unaffected."

"Don't flatter me," Ou Xiaolin mumbled with her eyes closed.

In the face of a lively, unaffected young woman, Luo Ke sank into his slightly unbridled reverie. The sleeping beauty was the kind of women that delighted and mesmerized Luo Ke. Her figure and smiling face evoked a sense of familiarity in him the moment they shook hands. At their homely wine party, the first sip of the Tsingtao beer plunged him into the retrospection of the past years. The vivid image of himself as a chubby teenager who always halted in front of the vaulting horse resurfaced in his mind. In the meanwhile, another Ou Xiaolin with bobbed hair in a nurse's uniform was smiling towards him in a room with blurred furnishings. It was as if Luo Ke were watching a movie starring Ou Xiaolin, and the story it told were about his personal experience. She (Ou Xiaolin) was wearing a swimsuit and smoking a cigarette, which seemed strange yet sweet, her skin tanned, like a Thai woman.

"She seemed like someone I knew in childhood," Luo Ke whispered to Yin Chu.

"It's the first time you've ever said two people are similar in the world."

"She was important to me. She was the subject of all my sexual fantasies back then."

"What's her name?" Yin Chu asked.

"I don't remember. She was a nurse and married early. Her husband was a swimming coach, a cousin of my mother. Once my mother told me to take a watch back from their home, and we only met once."

"Did you go through anything special?"

"No. She was walking around the room. It was fleeting, like a frame of a movie, and I fell for her," Luo Ke said with self-mockery.

"What about now?" Yin Chu pursued the matter.

"Oh, it's merely another old movie added to my collection."

"Nothing more than that?"
"I think."

3

That was far from the truth as there was another version of this significant movie other than Luo Ke's understatement. He never grew tired of watching it and would sometimes think that he could name it "The Swimming Pool." It took place in summer with the same main characters, and the style was impressionistic. The numerous bright spots in the water revealed the undulating waves of energy spreading out, suggesting the opposite of sexuality—the all-devouring death. But twenty years had passed, and in retrospect Luo Ke came to learn the destructive force of the gust of sexuality, the desolate ruins left after its sudden strike, the unpredictable trauma it caused, the despairing reconstruction of the refuge in his heart and the haunting old scenes that lingered on in a new relationship. In short, it carried more signs of the last hurrah, the imminent death. To this day helpless yearning and the analytical tendency of interpretation and exposition accompanied his review of the initial moment. It worked liked the English adverbial suffix, which gave moral uniformity to different meanings, and was at the same time an extension of the truth per se. The constant retrospection formed regular grooves in Luo Ke's brain, and the pendulum of memory frequently swung towards the end of interpretation. The impulse gradually faded away and carried those splendid pictures away with it in the end.

The youthful image of "Ou Xiaolin" beside the swimming pool never changed, though the relaxed manner in which she jumped from the one-meter springboard into the pool might be Luo Ke's imagination. He could not even recall whether her swimming stroke was the graceful breaststroke or the fastest freestyle. She swam towards Luo Ke from across the pool and stopped in front of him, adjusting her swimming cap. "Let me teach you," she said to the seven-year-old boy. It was the banal beginning of the old movie, different from the theme of a cut-out that bore the same name, created by Matisse two years before his death. Through the figures joyfully doing a spinning dive, Matisse the master bid farewell to the theme: the vigorous human body and animal in motion, the body cleansed of sins, and a terminal itself.

In Luo Ke's mind, women were dreamy with an everyday sense of lyricism. They never appeared with a transcendent quality; they were always there, unavoidable, and could never fit into any concept. They were like a ray of light in one's view, transient and yet captivating and unforgettable. They were worth one's life-long memory, reappearing in one's mind until they were changed by one's memory. Luo Ke knew that they were living somewhere in the world, having a life he did not know anything about, or perhaps they had died. It didn't matter. The point was that their images remained stable in Luo Ke's memory, catering to his needs and desires, while sometimes it was quite the opposite, as subtle changes were made to please the senses aesthetically. Women changed beautifully like music, though they might lead you to accumulated pain and sorrow when the melody ended.

Once a scene in childhood was connected with a special woman, it certainly carried a sense of fantasy and involved illusion and pacifism. But who could require a child, born in peacetime or partial wartime to be exact, to understand and react sensibly to slaughter, injustice, suffering of the unarmed and humans' painful and hopeless process of conquering nature with their limbs?

Luo Ke had no choice but to wait for his mental pictures to be changed in the future. They included both love and war, which were separated by space. Luo Ke was still able to see similarities effortlessly, though he seemed to remain undisturbed by their brutality and capriciousness, as if he had prepared himself for that.

The seven-year-old Luo Ke was big-boned and fair-skinned.

He was walking on the asphalt path to the swimming pool in a cotton crew-neck shirt, swinging his arms, his forehead oozing sweat. The pavement became sticky under the scorching summer sun, giving off an indelibly pungent smell. The walk contained nothing that helped to enhance the atmosphere in Luo Ke's imagination; it only provided a clue that had cooled down for his future recollection. The list of odors also included the smell of the pool water, bleaching powder and the bodies floating in front of him.

Luo Ke remembered how foolishly he swam back and forth under the water, bulging his eyes like goldfish and imagining that he was surrounded by swaying waterweeds and brilliant corals. What he saw was, however, the swimming coach peeing underwater. Little Luo Ke raised his head above the water in terror. The nurse swam towards him, and with a splash of water her husband put his arm around her from behind, making her smile to Luo Ke unfazed. She shook her head and her short hair swept the surface of the water. The silent scene shocked him as a blind shell with indifference and a strong sense of menace thrust in a strip of plough land in Vietnam.

4

The wide street was on a slope. The dark green body of a tramcar emerged from far away in the dusky curtain of rain. The doors and windows of the buildings along the street were all shut and seemed dusty through the bus window and reminded Luo Ke of waste depots and lethargic life. Not until now did he feel that they were in another city, a place he was unfamiliar with and had no interest in exploring.

"My home city," Ou Xiaolin said to him.

Luo Ke suddenly grew suspicious of this hasty trip. "I don't have time. You go," Yin Chu said to him, as if she were aware of his secret wish. Luo Ke felt the city had evoked a mixed feeling in him. It was like an exquisite sand table, where all his experiences and imaginations could be modeled; it was also like a museum which remained open to the past days and displayed them in an array with no obstruction.

Another tramcar emerged, pressing hard and slowly against the pavement. For a second, Luo Ke thought it was parked there, like a picture in his memory.

"I need to go to the Qiu Lin Company first," Ou Xiaolin said.

Luo Ke looked at him in confusion.

"My mother works there. I need to ask her for the key. Do you want to go with me? It's the most well-known department store here."

"No, it's not like I'm on a field trip."

"I forgot you work at a store too."

"It's fine. I can remind you at any time."

"I haven't been home for five years," Ou Xiaolin changed the subject.

"Have you ever felt homesick?"

"I don't know. People who occasionally go out will feel that they are away from all the chaos and trouble. But since I'm always away from home, it has become a quiet place in my mind."

"I've never been far away from home, until this time. I think home is the full package. It has everything you want and don't want," Luo Ke said.

The airport bus turned onto the avenue next to Stalin Square. It was raining, and several military men were taking pictures in the center of the square.

"Can I call you Qiao?" Ou Xiaolin suddenly asked before they got off the bus. She had asked the question already on the McDonnell airplane.

"Why?"

"I think the pronunciation suits you."

"Is it supposed to be my name or surname?"

"It's a nickname! Or pet name."

"Fine, then I'll call you ring lock."

"Why?"

"Just because. It's a temporary mark, and I might call you loop antenna after we get off."

"Right."

Ou Xiaolin took the keys from her mother and went to pick up Luo Ke on the pavement in front of the Qiu Lin Company. A big local man was inquiring of him about something, and he was trying to explain while imitating the man's accent. The big man seemed upset after listening to him for a while and left.

"He asked me whether I wanted any girls. He can provide a hotel room," Luo Ke reported to Ou Xiaolin who was walking towards him.

"You made that up."

"Yes, I did. Let's go."

Carrying their luggage, they walked in single file and went to a secluded backstreet after going through a narrow alley parked with bicycles.

"What's your mother like?" Luo Ke asked.

"What can an old lady be like?" Ou Xiaolin asked in reply.

"I mean she must have been happy to see you."

"She started crying behind the counter before I said anything."

"It can't be helped." Luo Ke found that he said something out of nowhere.

"My father died. It's been a year." Ou Xiaolin stopped walking and started crying on the pavement. "I didn't know. If I knew, I would have come back."

"What can I say to stop you from crying?"

"Nothing."

The rainwater flowed downwards along the lower sides of the street washed clean. It would be a perfect scene for Luo Ke to add into his collection of memories. For the first time Luo Ke experienced the shock that long-distance travel brought him and the strange feeling that the appearance of an unfamiliar city in a traveler's eyes was moist and dusty. In its stillness there were traces of revelry, which did not occur overnight but rather were scars left over a long period of evolution. They remained in the exposed scarlet mud, symbolizing unspeakable brutality and pain. The city unconsciously gave off a glimmer of dryness in the chilly drizzle at two in the afternoon. "The north," Luo Ke said to himself. Not until this moment did he understand the meaning of geography. This girl who kept sobbing under a tree on the pavement irrevocably withdrew from Luo Ke's romantic imagination. The beautiful figure of her standing in the rain suggested all the dimness of the past. "I barely know her," Luo Ke said.

The scenery in Ou Xiaolin's hometown made her appear more exposed in Luo Ke's eyes, but at the same she became as mysterious as an image in the mirror, which happened in an instant. By the crying and the whimpering of her soul, she told her deceased father who gave her life everything she had experienced. Her absent look added to Luo Ke's loneliness of being in another city away from home and revealed the blindness of the trip.

Some women were products of life, whose nature included the inclination to live in captivity, while some were shaped by roaming around, who were born with the wish to live in self-exile. Despite the difference in their way of life and experiences, they had all been through hardships and were capable of making a scene in their own domain. Luo Ke was not an expert in distinguishing between them and was often at a loss when facing those women with different looks on their face. He was a "permanent beginner" whose eyes were burned by glamour in the realm of phenomena.

5

At night, Luo Ke and Ou Xiaolin were drinking tea at the small round table in the living room. Both of them appeared a little weary in the dim light. Luo Ke leaned against the chair and listened to Ou Xiaolin recount the history of the city D, letting words like the Soviet Red Army, Belarusian prostitutes and Manchuria accompany his weariness. After a while, when she was introducing the Russian style building they were now in with the general and superficial explanations like a tour guide, she touched upon her family and unavoidably mentioned her father again. To steer clear of the sad topic, Ou Xiaolin started talking about her parents' relationship with a longing tone, trying to dilute the grief with her discursive memory of trivialities.

Ou Xiaolin took out a thick album with a satin cover from an antique rosewood cabinet embossed with a design of Rohdea japonica. Luo Ke was able to detect a trace of musty smell, which he could not ignore, in the overwhelming odor of camphor. The cover of the album appeared extremely dim, and the dust had been stationed in the gaps between every fiber and blended extremely well with the gloomy landscape. Ou Xiaolin flipped the pages and suddenly stopped to show Luo Ke a photo, "This was my grandfather."

The middle aged man respectfully referred to as "my grandfather" by Ou Xiaolin looked handsome and courageous and was, inexplicably, wearing a Russian military uniform with many buttons on the chest. His eyebrows were knitted, with noticeable anxiety in his firmness. The backdrop was a street of ice and snow in Harbin, and a group of trunks of different styles and sizes were piled next to him on the ground.

In the twenties, some unidentified Russian exiles were going to the American Continent by way of Harbin, and they once deposited their luggage with Ou Xiaolin's grandfather. When they came to retrieve their suitcases in a flurry, they often left something as a reward. Among those keepsakes which could not be measured by money were old Russian uniforms and a fine copy of poems by Lermontov.

The most astonishing gift, however, was an infant girl. Those fidgety, nameless exiles disappeared with no explanation on a cold night of thaw and never came back again. The mixed-blood girl who was mysteriously abandoned later married Ou Xiaolin's father.

Ou Xiaolin's mother was devastated by her birth. There was no way to confirm whether her father was Lithuanian or Belorussian. She did not know what happened in that time of turbulence between some Russian exile and some girl in Harbin. What other stories did their long-gone transient love bring to this world? Perhaps she could only use Lermontov's everlasting lines as an annotation to her birth, "A short love is vexing, and a permanent love's just a myth."

Overshadowed by the history which would never come to light, her own relationship became a boring real-life fake subordinate to imagination. Since the day she was able to manipulate her imagination, she had been indulging herself in endless fiction and hypothesis. Such complementary fabrication of a healing nature gradually morphed into a necessity.

She grew more and more introverted and taciturn, lengthy discussions replaced by her fits of sobbing. She buried herself in words, with her body motions almost reduced to iconography, and eventually lost her interest in sex completely.

As a daughter, she was adopted; as a wife, she had grown up with her husband; as a mother, she was the epitome of sentimentality for Ou Xiaolin. Her ability to retrieve emotional memories was comparable to that of a well-trained professional actress, as she could wail over her adversities at any time anywhere. Objectively speaking, Ou Xiaolin had learned a lot in such an environment. Her sensitivity, paranoia, self-torture and narcissism were all formed under her mother's influence. Her untraceable romantic birth provided infinite ways of fabrication for Ou Xiaolin's mental activity. The ability to make something up out of thin air passed onto the daughter through whining and crying.

6

In Ou Xiaolin's mother's view, Luo Ke was no better than a vagrant. The eccentric, listless young man who always let his hair swing on his forehead seemed more than dubious. Besides, her daughter had never talked about him before he suddenly showed up, holding her daughter's hand, which reminded the old lady of her past and was all the more reason for her to be on guard. In the deep of the night, the paranoid mother, listening to the whispers from the living room, tossed and turned in bed and felt sorrow surging up in her. She cried on and off like a baby, grumbling and babbling a meaningless monologue. It lingered in the room like a piece of music and upset the already downhearted Ou Xiaolin. She started to walk around the room, making noises by kicking the things in her way like desks and chairs as a response to her mother's explicit emotional expression. Luo Ke once and again beseeched her to stop her irregular walking and contention with a woman obsessed with her memories. He compared Ou Xiaolin's mother at the moment to a vulture, as she was interested in anything rotten in her memory. Ou Xiaolin was displeased with the vivid metaphor and felt like reproaching him vehemently. Oddly, in that instant, she sensed something next to the nature of her life. She realized that she was always making friends with some guy in haste and then having a thorough talk with them about many things in detail in a very short time. The atmosphere was always amiable and they would always reach consensus on some topics they were both interested in. She had no idea why she excelled in such things. She shared her principles and experiences with the other without reservation, though she was keenly aware that she deceived the other as well as herself. Such subtle moments of introspection were not uncommon in Ou Xiaolin's life. Every time she thought of this, she would be aroused outside in, and Luo Ke's face was the typical and only image in her mind in such a moment ruled by desire. She urged herself to be more infatuated with his voice and countenance and to distinguish his scent in the air. The temperature of her slightly dark skin rose imperceptibly, her hands and feet still cold. But of course at the moment, Luo Ke was not holding them. The exertion of travelling and his unfamiliarity with the city came over him in the moonlight after rain. In the haziness it warmed his weariness and embellished his consciousness which was quickly fading away with star-shaped ornaments. The dreamland he was entering was as tranquil as the night sky, and among all the serenity there was hidden excitement as mysterious as space travel. The sense of vicissitude when listening to the stories just now transformed into the weariness which was falling away. Like a perplexed lover whose soul was taken away by the beautiful figure among the rosebushes in the garden, he was lost in a deeper trance.

7

On a clear day like the second day after they arrived in the city D, when they were breathing the fresh air from the sea, Luo Ke's heart was filled with tenderness. He gazed at the shade of trees cordially appealing to him, and Yin Mang's face emerged from the depths of his mind. The image was so clearly exposed in the radiance of pure affection that the shadow blurred by the flow of time glimmered with benevolence. Her sincere intonation and unshakable faith with which she calmly stated her disappointment, indifference and weariness with love chilled Luo Ke to the marrow. For the first time he saw the horror that resulted from the sorrow and the anxiety in love. Astounded by his vulnerability, he was ashamed to experience the anxious hesitation on the brink of emotional breakdown, followed by fits of headache and nausea. The two emotions mixed with each other, gradually solidified into one piece, and eventually morphed into something hard and solid, which was covered with blemishes on the surface while radiating on the inside.

What haunted him was not some residence of the soul that banished him. To this day he was still unable to figure out its true meaning. Sometimes he felt it was a storybook that had been torn apart. Though the pages were disorganized, destroyed and abandoned, its content was endowed with a more mysterious order.

Their contact was changed from the skin, breath and even desire within reach to more distant connection. The few words found in these fragments revealed the once fiery lust, and by cobbling what little left together, he managed to relive those reversed scenes and moments. The memories created an intriguing sense that everything developed in an endless circle. What faded into the distance started coming back along an invisible path, and those moments of rapture would be lost forever instead of reviving somewhere else, while those who enjoyed them would continue to exist and head for a new place of withering accompanied by their memories.

Luo Ke was often unable to tell where he was, as both repose and depression would leave him at a loss with no sense of direction or judgment, let alone the technical tricks like analyzing or adapting to the circumstance. The past was never internalized as experience. The only thing he had been relying on for a long time was his impulse, sometimes with the help of the environment and accidents. Of course, he would sometimes consider it a superior way of living. The sweet smell of boiled milk wafted through the narrow door of the kitchen; the TV transmitting towers standing still on the distant mountain were visible from the back window above the stair winders; several lightweight cars spiraled up the road, leaving it spotlessly sparkling under the sunshine. Luo Ke cautioned himself against being overwhelmed by the emotions evoked by a single scene or forgetting the absurdity of the trip. Milk was milk. He should not associate it with the warmth of family. Ou Xiaolin got up early, washed her face, and bustled around only because you were her guest. Otherwise she might still have been in bed, disheveled. Luo Ke was amused when thinking of Ou Xiaolin's peculiar sleeping posture. Ou Xiaolin, who was drunk then, lay in Yin Chu's messy bed with her limbs spreading out as if reading an ode with her left hip sticking out a little as if introducing an African dance move into the classical ballet, occupying the whole bed with her body and even her facial expression. Ou Xiaolin's arbitrary sleeping posture made Yin

Chu retreat. "She can't possibly be anyone's wife. No man can lie in the same bed with her," Luo Ke concluded on the spot, "but she could be many men's lover."

8

Ou Xiaolin announced in the afternoon that a small party that would be both joyful and melancholic would take place at seven, with many chubby guests coming. When the night fell, deserted by the smiling hostess, Luo Ke had to sit on a chair in the corner as a part-time onlooker who frequently rose to pour tea for guests on her command. Most of the time Luo Ke pretended to be browsing through a book named *The World Factbook* published in 1956. A retired military man who was later said to have "great capacity for liquor" complained in a loud voice the moment he came in, "What a dull atmosphere! Where's the spirit of revolution?" Luo Ke put back the book on the shelf and saw Ou Xiaolin wink at him. "Drink and eat! Drink and eat!" the great-capacity man started yelling again at the table. A small group of women with heavy makeup (who proved to be Ou Xiaolin's classmates back in the primary school) cheered towards the hostess on the stairs, "Darling, darling!" Then they explained to Luo Ke that she liked them addressing her that way. After that the arrival of a man with his hair parted to one side made everything less casual and added a bourgeoisie element to the party. He talked at length about the so-called inferiority complex of small countries while smoking his foreign cigarette, who was then dubbed "White House Press Secretary" by the women on the spot for his enthusiasm about the American presidents in the history. "Leaders," he said, "my ambition is to become a leader." "Are you all right? Were you drunk already before you came here?" a woman interrupted. Luo Ke wanted to take *The World Factbook* back from the shelf when Ou Xiaolin walked over and pressed a glass of wine on him. "Come over and talk with them." "In this age," the White House

Press Secretary said, "people are left with nothing to abandon, and then they start to abandon their lovers and wives." "Are you OK?" people shouted at him. "Abandon love. Yes, this trend was a continuation of the abandoning society as a collective noun ten years ago. People went from selflessness to extreme selfishness." "He's totally out of his mind," the audience explained to each other. "And undoubtedly those reactionaries became martyrs. Of course, they would repent someday. But there was no uniformity like that between the former and the former of the former in the following age." The speaker had barely finished the sentence before he slid under the table. "What's wrong with him? Why did he say such things?" they asked Ou Xiaolin. "I have no idea. Perhaps he's unwell."

The women continued talking in a loud voice and ignored the man under the table. He seemed relaxed and comfortable lying in the shadow, with the look of a mischievous child who had just played a prank.

Luo Ke came back to his chair and sipped at his cup. Cheers broke out from time to time where the women huddled together, who then looked around in surprise as if worrying that someone might know their secrets.

Ou Xiaolin came over and said to Luo Ke, "They are talking about you. Do you want to know?"

"Tell me when we go to bed."

Ou Xiaolin seemed surprised and looked at him, "I don't think the party is going to end any time soon."

"I'll wait."

They stared at each other for a while, expressionless. In a moment, they had a new agreement, as if it were discovered by pure accident, though the process had lasted a long time. They did not realize how long it had been, just as they only remembered the moment they left, the moment they left a melancholy city or melancholy itself. There was nothing but melancholy between one kind of intimacy and another. And now, he was awaken by the waiting he was conscious of. He found himself waiting, but the confirmation made him anxious. The guests started dancing. Husbands and wives, fiancés and fiancées, people who fell in love and the unprepared were all in place. They were like a group of structuralists familiar with classification, who would never make mistakes in such things. Agile in mind and body, they would find their place effortlessly no matter where they came from or where they went. The way Ou Xiaolin gently swayed in her partner's arms made Luo Ke tremble and immediately look out of the window. Ou Xiaolin's mother was alone in darkness, collecting clothes in slow motion. Luo Ke watched her stagger and felt lost. People look for habitation like birds. They gather together, twittering; they rise to get food; they fly to have a taste of the air and get hurt; they fly back, fall and die on the ground. When do they think? During the chitchat? Luo Ke found himself more and more ridiculous. He forced himself to look back at the people dancing instead of making a cruel analogy out of his anxiety. Ou Xiaolin was talking with the White House Press Secretary, as if they were exchanging opinions about some self-evident issues. As a result, the negotiation broke down and the man lay back against the chair.

Ou Xiaolin suddenly shouted to him, and everyone paused, except that the music continued. Ou Xiaolin waved her hand, "Forget it." Everyone started moving again, though the music stopped. "Fine," Luo Ke said to himself. He rose, dragged the White House Press Secretary out of the house and left him on the cold stairs, "Who will take him away?"

"It's already twelve!" Ou Xiaolin's mother came into the room and announced in a white nightgown covered with pale blue flowers and a nightcap. She sounded as if dubbing for a monster in a puppet show. Luo Ke rose and walked out.

"It's too late. Let's go home," people said. They quietly walked across the yard to the street. Ou Xiaolin insisted on walking with them and joined the drunken group, holding Luo Ke's arm. Without the hubbub in the day, the midnight breeze made them feel peaceful. Someone suggested they sing a song on such a beautiful night. Seeing that Luo Ke was not in the mood, Ou Xiaolin said to them, "Save your energy and we'll sing another day." Then they parted at the corner as if they were truly saving their energy.

There was nobody but Luo Ke and Ou Xiaolin on the street. "I think we should run back home," Ou Xiaolin suggested. The stars remained still in the night sky, or at least they seemed to be. They started running on the pavement. "I've never run towards a woman like now." "Neither have I." "What?" "Run towards a man." "It's terrible." "Indeed."

9

"Where do you want to go tomorrow?" Ou Xiaolin asked.

"I want to take a tramcar ride or just stay at home," Luo Ke said.

"You like tramcars?"

"They remind me of something. I don't know. Nostalgia, I guess."

"I've got many postcards collected on my own. Do you want to see?"

"Right now? I can't." Luo Ke kissed Ou Xiaolin's eyes, smiling.

"All right, I'll stop talking." She held him more closely to her chest.

It was quiet at night. There were only some untraceable, intermittent sounds that came from far away, which added to the indistinct sweetness. At such moments, Luo Ke and Ou Xiaolin would hold their breath, as if listening to the soothing and bewildering sounds of the still night.

"What's that sound?" Luo Ke asked.

"Your hallucination."

"You didn't hear that?"

"I only heard your breath."

Their disjointed conversation accompanied their sex with ease and sometimes smoothly integrated itself with it. From the beginning, Luo Ke sensed that every second contained homely margin for words, which was inconspicuously delivered by her continuous movement, as if she were saying, "If silence means enjoyment, words mean praise." Every time when the conversation ended, Luo Ke would suddenly feel jilted, as if it were a temporary shelter for his soul. And he was saved from the brink of death by a new conversation, elated as if he found out the ability to think for the first time. Soon he was lost again in his maze and chose to linger there. On such a night of tenderness, the language of her soft body was spoken under his close gaze. Her wildness and reserve carried passion and pervasive indifference like deep-sea skin. Her bones, the folded parts of her body that supported her, the smooth skin, the coy, reddish birthmark, and moles scattered on her smooth skin like grains of salt—all revealed her infinite longing. The collapse like her suck and appeal vanished in a second. As if following a lead to pleasure, Luo Ke eventually buried his head in her soft black hair. "The fragrance," Luo Ke thought.

At night, the flow of time seemed to have a clear direction. Flooding in like the tide, memories of the past days touched upon the fountain in his heart and illustrated, with the warmth of a ray of sunshine, the sudden changes, abandonment and betrayal in his love which suddenly struck like a disease. The despair that gradually permeated his life like water drops presented Yin Mang's image in front of his eyes again. This time she became as pale as a light stroke on the edge of the landscape. It was as if she only existed and appeared to make Luo Ke pine for her and feel the coldness in regret, as well as to transform the sorrow into a still life for permanent appreciation. He asked himself about every detail of Yin Mang's departure like a fool. Every scene of the doom of their affection was included without exception in his cherished, endless memory.

It was raining on and off on that autumn day. Luo Ke

read one of the letters from Yin Mang and then some of André Dhôtel's *L'horizon*. He made his confused mind shuttle between the two as if the mystic writer's work was the annotation of Yin Mang's heartless letters. Rain pattered on the window like disorganized drumbeats, tickling down like tears. Meanwhile, Yin Mang and Sun Shu began their honeymoon on a trip to Guilin. "I said that I couldn't make any promise of anything at any time." Luo Ke sat in the sofa cross-legged, listening to the patter of the rain. He thought every word in that letter came from a woman he barely knew, who had walked through his heart towards another man. Luo Ke was missing her all the time, which he wondered whether she knew. Not until then did Luo Ke realize that Yin Mang's leaving him showed him how much he loved her. He found it hard to express his feelings. Often he would wake up from a sound sleep and felt acutely the touch of her skin. He felt as if he had lost a wife he had lived with for years, and it broke his heart to lose her youth, petulance, beauty, and unpredictability.

In the short period of time brimming with their mutual attraction, passion and desire, her kisses and touches infiltrated his skin and evoked his affection. And at this moment, in the dim light, the space around Luo Ke, which they shared in common, stared at him indifferently, asking about the woman who filled the room with her illusory presence, "What is she doing?"

"I love you," Luo Ke thought. But he no longer expected the stupid sentence to be heard by Yin Mang. It would never be heard. The ears had been shut, waiting for another source. He was only confiding to the image of Yin Mang that he borrowed in despair. The wish, which was gently vibrating, was only a prayer, a Mass and a requiem.

"Are you all right?" Ou Xiaolin looked at Luo Ke, confused. She had no idea why he still looked absent-minded. His unusual quietness frightened her. The light from his eyes was either because of sex or because of someone who would come back from the dead sometime. "You are really inexplicable. From a clinical perspective—don't laugh—I mean in medical terms, I'm afraid you've got Ernest Syndrome."

"What?" Luo Ke did not understand.

"Sexual dysfunction."

"Boring."

"True."

10

From a microcosmic standpoint, Ou Xiaolin was a carrier of numerous terms and concepts, which were all keepsakes from her lovers, whether abstruse or plain. Normally they were given to her in a joyful atmosphere but sometimes in rude curses. Ou Xiaolin was always ready to throw them out, as if reciting lines. Her simplified way of using them made them resonate, which made the audience back off. At such moments she would be devastated, thinking that she had no idea how to turn things around without a favorable wind. She began her self-inquiry again when Luo Ke fell asleep.

Deep down in Ou Xiaolin's heart, there had been the image of a gentleman, who was tall, mature, well-mannered and amiable, though Ou Xiaolin had never made out his face. Such a man who could not even be described in detail influenced her life and helped her to remain detached from the life she detested. Every man in her life had a figure similar to him, but unfortunately, every time they turned around, they would always give away something different from the idolized man.

It was near dawn and the room was draped in a grayish haze. Ou Xiaolin suddenly rose up and started shaking Luo Ke. "Please get up. I want to talk to you." She shook his head with force.

"Stop it! I beg you! You're killing me," Luo Ke implored her with his eyes closed.

"What?"

"I'm not in my right mind now. Please let me sleep. Oh my."

"It's OK. Talking helps to clear your head." She patted his face, as if turning on a switch or giving a secret signal.

"All right. I'll get up." Luo Ke raised his head one inch higher on the pillow. "Now I've sat up. Please let me go back to sleep."

"All right, all right." Ou Xiaolin stopped patting him, "You can still lie in bed but you must answer my question."

"But darling, it's not even dawn yet."

"You are right. That's why we need to hurry and finish this before dawn."

"Why?" Luo Ke's eyes widened.

"Look, you are just awake, but I didn't sleep all night."

"Why?"

"I just couldn't. I couldn't fall asleep. Do you understand?"

"OK. I'll sleep on the sofa."

"Please."

"Is this what you want?"

"Maybe I should go."

"I won't stop you," he mumbled for a while and gradually quieted down as if he had said everything he wanted to say. He turned around cozily and fell asleep, his face on the blue pillow towel embroidered with cranes. She picked up the maroon blanket and groped her way to the sofa. The conversation ended before it even started, as if they had nothing to talk in the dimness and thus discussed it and had a conversation about the conversation itself. The moment her palm touched the cold leather of the sofa, she felt that this kind of conversation was the only kind she could possibly live with. Apart from that, what kind of conversation could have taken place in this room suffused with the smell of tobacco, liquor and sweat? Didn't the body she was growing familiar with have the compatibility she had longed for? Didn't she explicitly accept all the caresses that he gave her without reservation? She no longer despaired that it was only a temporary thing as she used to. Didn't the intimacy assure her the peace that transcended satisfaction? She wrapped herself tight with a blanket, pressing her skin against the prickly texture, the sofa squeaking under her. Though everything was still in a haze, the grayness behind the curtains began to lighten, and a sense of satisfaction rose in Ou Xiaolin's belated sleepiness. She vaguely felt proud of her feminine senses, with which she spied on her weak, tempted body during the dizziness of kissing. There was something dark and horrifying about it, like a silhouette. With a sense of decay and persistent yearning, it slid down into the soil with little resistance like raindrops on the branch of a palm tree and received a full explanation. With her sight blocked by the closed eyelids, she was eventually filled with tiredness and somehow aware that she was taking a rest.

The sky finally revealed its brilliance after remaining in obscurity for a long time. Ou Xiaolin, who was sound asleep on the sofa, still sensed the light outside despite the closed curtains. She constantly changed her positions unconsciously and even used her hand to block the morning light that streamed through the gap onto her face. Luo Ke was awake and not sure whether it was his sleep or Ou Xiaolin's that changed her anxious look. He asked with such a friendly tone that surprised himself, "Are you awake?"

"Leave me alone." A knowing warning came out of the blanket.

"I'm not taking revenge. You go on sleeping." Luo Ke paused for about a second, "I think I should have a cigarette. Ah, here it is. OK, what should I do now? Well, I should plot my novel ..."

"Shut up!" Ou Xiaolin suddenly sat bolt upright on the sofa and cried.

"I didn't mean to disturb you." Luo Ke stared at the grumpy woman for a while and asked, "Do you want a cigarette? I can bring one to you if you do."

"I've decided to hate you." Ou Xiaolin moved a little on the sofa, making some room. "You slept with me once and you already started talking to me like that."

"I'm not gay," Luo Ke explained.

"What do you mean?" Ou Xiaolin took the cigarette from

his hand and had a puff.

"I can't just get up and start expressing my love even before brushing my teeth. Now would you share your blanket with me? Thank you. Give me my cigarette, please. Ah, great. Well, let's talk now. You wanted to talk, right?"

"Now?" Ou Xiaolin said peevishly, wrinkling her nose, "I don't know what we should talk about before you brush your teeth to avoid raising suspicion about our sexuality."

"There, there." Luo Ke patted her head, "I was just joking."

They smoked the cigarette in turn until there was only the butt burnt on the edge left. Luo Ke aimed at a glass ashtray on the table and tossed the butt.

"How lucky I am!" Luo Ke said with pride. He pulled the blanket up to his neck and cleared his throat loudly, "It's so cold."

It was indeed a cold morning. Even the rustling of people walking on the street gave off a sense of chilliness. It seemed to be a most ordinary morning, though many things of significance happened or perished somewhere far away from them, which would be recorded by some other people in a solemn way. There must be some people crying as the most important time in their life had come, while many more were just brushing their teeth in a hurry. At this moment, someone passed by the window, and the sound his leather shoes made on the fallen leaves only affected Luo Ke slightly. He knew where he was, though he did not know why.

11

Luo Ke idled about the whole morning and suffered from boredom. He had been dragging his lanky body around the room, as he was tired of seeing the allegedly exquisite scenery of this coastal city. Though the old tramcars still went into his sight from time to time, evoking his imagination, somehow he preferred to enjoy the limited view through his window—the blotchy low wall, the little wooden gate with peeling paint, and the unknown small tree that was barely alive. Luo Ke tried many times to collect the evidence on them that evoked his reveries, as if they were real. At last a peculiar sense of sleepiness prompted him to sit down and write to Yin Chu. "Between Ou Xiaolin and me, she is more like a traveler, always heading out. She meets all kinds of people and sometimes even brings them back. I just want to sleep. I feel a strong sense of sleepiness 24 hours a day." Luo Ke thought Yin Chu might be able to sympathize with his lethargic state. "Please forgive me for writing to you. I'll tell you my motive. In this city I don't know anything about, I miss Yin Mang terribly. I have a weird feeling that I came all the way here just to think of her. I'm studying everything around me to see what on earth is making me feel this way."

While he was writing, his pining for Yin Mang grew more and more strong. He put down his pen and held his head like a terrified child. Haunted by the feeling, he started talking to Yin Mang, though not ostensibly. All of a sudden he realized that he was continuing writing the letter to the dead. "Is she dead?" Luo Ke asked himself. What a sweet question! It secretly linked the underlying concern with the unconfirmed death. If this fine lady really died, people should focus on her remains, as they would find her repose, her impeccable serenity and the delicacy of her fingers when they saw her in eternal sleep. Her words as gentle as spring thaw would always be able to penetrate one's heart. "When I was with her," Luo Ke wrote in a new paragraph, "it was like I had dermatographism. My skin was so hot and sensitive that I thought the blood would spurt from my vessels. But why am I telling you this? Just because you was once hopelessly in love with a black man? The pain he brought you, the real pain, the pain of love, was far more than that from the prison. Right now how much I want to hold you both in my arms! I love you two sisters with gratitude, for you accepted my disastrous, lunatic love successively like martyrs. Now I'll rephrase it in a less exaggerative and figurative way. You two helped me and saved me from paralysis. Your love was so divine (how much wretchedness and bitterness I felt in this word) that the worst obscenities in the world could not detract from it. It was like the mesmerizing view before your eyes at dusk, subtle and transient. This is how I love you, but who believes it? Do you? You have given half your heart to the liar and the other half to the prison, and in all, to darkness. Does Yin Mang? Is there anything on earth that is more lasting than my pining heart? Her death? My death will surpass it and will last longer with more stillness." Luo Ke suddenly stopped writing and walked around the room, as his emotions interfered with his train of thought. The sunlight outside the window streamed down on the streets and brought a sense of warmth to the fresh air. He could even hear the rumbling of a tramcar though it was a street away from him. It drew his attention like a hallucination and brought back one or two seasons in the past, some episodes of life, and several chapters of some woman's life story, which all surrounded it and knocked on his heart. The theme he could not let go of was like a melody of fate that was played in the air in harmony with his heart, and whenever he walked into it, he was able to recognize it instantly without effort. The women's suffering and their natural charm when they swayed gently made for their attractive appearance and made the motif of their life the attempt to free themselves from gravity. Suicide under the wheels, as an urban scene that had disappeared, implanted its sensation in Luo Ke's memory and lingered in his chaotic imagination. The dim light transformed it into a sign, a soft object that fell with the wind. It surpassed emotions with its material properties, affected Luo Ke's mind as a pure spatial image and left him lost in its microscopic structure. He walked to the bed and inadvertently saw a soft hair on the bed sheet. He felt a vague, mild sorrow in him. He thought it was like sailors' rigging knives and teenage girls' accessories, which were used for assaulting the despairing travelers and their feelings to make them sink deeper. He came back to the desk to continue writing, breathing steadily with a calm look on the face, his body slightly hunched in the warm light. "Few people are able to get rid of their craziness." He pictured Yin Chu reading the letter with a perplexed look. "Especially those who are not good at lying, because lying helps to detox our body to some extent. You are wrong if you think I'm alluding to something or someone. Please don't ask me to explain it to you. I shall tell you how I fight it when I feel like going crazy. I once told myself that if I don't do drugs, I should read Karen Horney, imagine that I have neurosis, and study all those chapters about anxiety, fear, hostility, sensitivity to rejection, recoiling from competition, guilt, masochism, exhaustion, conflict, chronic, and partial dying. I can't find anything better than this to kill time."

"I read with great excitement, hearing my heart pounding, the sound of which drowned everything else. It had an unparalleled sense of hugeness, like a carefully folded sleeping bag being inflated from within. When it was almost done, I was stuffed into it, suffocated. I was like a wrapped parcel."

"I ask you again not to make me explain. Everything, from the beginning to the end. There is no explanation." Luo Ke continued, "You've never asked me how I choose my underpants. Stay that way. Don't be obsessed with color, size, texture or shape. Attachment to those properties has nothing to do with the sense of belongingness that keeps developing and manifesting itself, or with the retreat from the outside world to the inner world. It is purely a preference instead of an interest."

Luo Ke stopped again. He rose up from the chair but instead of leaving, he sat on the desk and continued to scribble on the paper. He hoped that Ou Xiaolin would come in and interrupt him by shouting or throwing something at him or dragging his clothes. But nobody appeared in the quietness, and he still had to live with his anxiety.

Travel, a useless form of migration, left him more focused on the past and its meaning. Hebrew prophets had illuminated this. At this moment, the change of space, like a violinist's changing positions, complemented the pervasive southern melancholy.

12

Late at night, Ou Xiaolin appeared in the soft lighting of the room when the noises far and near gradually faded away. It was almost dawn. Luo Ke looked anxious, as he had waited for and cursed her for a long time on the sofa. He pricked up his ears and noticed the light of joy in her clear eyes, which could be produced at midnight by nothing except alcohol and sex.

Luo Ke wondered why she came back now, but he immediately felt like a thief in a hotel, who lived in one room and coveted another. He stood up and walked over to her in inexplicable anguish. With a strong sense of uncertainty about what he was to her, he didn't know what to ask and felt as sad as an actor with no role to play.

"I was really worried, seriously," Luo Ke said.

"I was not far away," she said in a candid tone, as if she was permitted by the night to come and go as she pleased. "You are observing me now. How unusual! Why are you looking at me that way? Hey, wake up. I'm your friend. Do you hear me?" she asked anxiously.

"Too late," he said.

"What?"

"You came back too late." He said calmly, "You should have come back around noon. After that point, it wouldn't make any difference when you came back."

"Don't be so dejected, as if I had made some mistake."

Luo Ke did not reply. His dejected expression turned a little odd, as if the word had reminded him of something.

She loved the man in front of her with all her heart. The love was not stable, but there was something hidden in its elusiveness. She loved his appearance, his layered hair and the sense of convergence when his slightly short-sighted eyes tried to focus. When they were alone, he tended to exert a traumatic influence on her. Both of them were sensitive. A fleeting glance, the quality of the voice, the slightest change in tone and even the moisture level of skin were detectible. It was easy to leave him, but he would leave a scar in the depths of her heart that would take a long time to heal. In this way, to forget him, instead of how, became the problem. He was different from anyone else she knew, though only in some trivial aspects. Most people lived all of the four changing seasons, but he only lived in one. He was dead on the ground most of the time, but every year, he was reborn, which was the reason for his sadness as well as his youth. The refreshing charm emanated from him delighted her, as knowledge delighted the mind, without any sense of heaviness. For that she was devoted to him, thereby gaining more self-respect and happiness, as if she had been doing some fulfilling work.

"I came back late. That's true, but nothing more." She walked briskly across the room to the bathroom, where she stuck out her head and said, "I like you. Don't you know that?" She didn't wait for Luo Ke's answer, "I don't know how to put this. For some time, or right now, I can't feel a sense of intimacy with anyone but you. I just can't. It's possible in theory but my body doesn't allow it. Do you understand? From head to toe."

Ou Xiaolin didn't turn on the light in the bathroom, perhaps because she could not stand the light of the 15-watt bulb. She flossed meticulously in the darkness, as if it were some kind of secret work in which she would establish a tacit understanding with someone.

Luo Ke thought she must have drunk too much. She once said to him that she liked to act like a drunken, foul-mouthed vixen who came back home late and didn't bother taking off the shoes before collapsing on the bed. She said it in such a way as if she were thinking of a movie in which she had played a role.

She thought the best way for a woman to avoid being taken for simple-minded was excessive drinking, which would make her seem experienced. Smoking was nothing like drinking. It was at best the icing on the cake, a highly suggestive embellishment.

Ou Xiaolin came out of the bathroom and walked over to Luo Ke, who was sitting on the sofa. She cupped his face in her hands and whispered, "If you don't feel like sleeping. Let's drink, OK?"

She apparently felt that her words touched him. There was a sheen of wetness in his eyes with well-controlled tenderness, which was a peculiar look of a man addicted to reveries. It seemed to have come from regret, guilt, even a slight bewilderment, a combination of compulsion and habit, the inside of which was like light reflected by a mirror.

"I think we should reintroduce ourselves to each other." He said, "I think we should have met when we were alone, not the way we did in real life. It should be more accidental."

He lifted up his eyes, staring at her, and saw the weary look on her face that would only appear in a close-up shot. "I think we are similar." He wanted to continue, but she interrupted him.

"No, we are totally different."

Luo Ke listened to her expectantly.

"I often cried in front of the camera without any reason. Though it was a requirement, it had nothing to do with anyone else. I like crying in front of other people, and making movies is just an excuse. I need to be surrounded by people and things. I can't even imagine being alone, but you don't need anyone. I saw that in you last night. You like being alone, being accompanied by your own voice, image and secrets. Your need for others eventually manifests itself as your need for no one."

"If you are right, then I am a reclusive idiot."

"I don't know if you are an idiot or not. I just know that I need more happiness. Not the happiness achieved by racking my brains. It should come from cuisine, exquisite clothes, lipsticks and people's attention."

Luo Ke understood that she was seeking satisfaction in the same way she was seeking love, as if the two were the same thing. She needed a verb, an inclination. She needed love that came from the inside or the outside, without asking for return or reverberation. He was different. He longed for mutual affection, which was intertwined and overlapping. Each response was closer. Therefore it was also feeble and needed shelter; it was overly frequent and thus illusory. He thought she was real, like porcelain, and at the same time showed that he fully appreciated her fragility. She, or women like her, was naturally challenging. They were committed to and gifted in perceiving and foreseeing ambiguity, which made them glow with inalienable charm and sorrow.

"Perhaps," Luo Ke said, "you can find something that says a lot in my experience."

"Don't tell me your story. If I ever asked, that was my mistake. Your story is no different from others', if you just change the time, places and characters. If it really were that extraordinary, wouldn't it be better that the characters remained anonymous?"

"I think I made a mistake." He said after a moment of silence, "There is no transition between two ways. You can only end it in the way you started it, either for one part or the whole."

"I don't understand."

"Either words or sex."

"You are being too absolute. You know this sentence itself is a transition."

13

"She." Who is she? Luo Ke asked himself. Is she Yin Mang, Xiang An, Liu Yazhi, Yin Chu, or Ou Xiaolin; or, is it someplace like Sidney, New York, Macau, or some domestic costal city? Who is he then? The art designer at a store who had two thousand five hundred yuan (approximately 555 US dollars) and a plane ticket with him, or a blindage in some jungle on the Indochinese Peninsula, or simply the camouflage on the antiaircraft artillery.

She and he and their relationship were clearly marked on the music score like notes and melody. Once played accurately, it would immediately demonstrate its illusiveness. She went broad and never turned back, regardless of the loneliness and the possibility of dying in another country. Her fine, delicate features defenselessly demonstrated her fragile elegance. On one summer night, her picture came from abroad, in which she seemed passionate and intellectually lethargic with her eyes and swollen lips. Her alluring coyness turned into hesitation, as if the foreign land had changed her overnight. Her remarkable youth and all the signs of indeterminateness were nowhere to be found; there was already the loneliness of an adult on her. The only detectable smile lay in the fine lines that extended from the corners of her mouth. This part he knew well, though it was only in a picture. "What about me?" Luo Ke thought of himself, "I was among the first to go abroad in our generation in the sixties, to the Red River. And then what? Back to my homeland, of course." Could he talk about anything else, after experiencing this southward trip? "No one knows my dream back then was to be strolling on a street there, in Hanoi, not in America or Australia."

My Hanoi. Many times Luo Ke wanted to write a novel about two people who fell in love at first sight in that setting, about the short-lived, unrealistic love that took place in the fury of war and was closely related to his initial fantasy. In that place which he had never been to, in those days that never existed, he met a dark-skinned Vietnamese girl with an alluring figure in the Duras style. They talked with each other with ambiguous gestures, as if describing the halo in front of their eyes. They exchanged soft words of love, which were not interpreted and thus nonsensical, in the rainy season in Dong Thap Muoi. All of this never happened, but they were not less real than the love that he experienced later in his life. It was as precious and reliable as oil palm, cinnamon, camphor and teakwood, emanating the tempting fragrance of the Annamite Range as the corn, sugarcane and coffee did. Then a tropical monsoon, however, blew them all away. The novel never came into being. Never. Many of Luo Ke's young comrades died in their position, and he lived with survivor guilt. When a great number of deaths took place in a concrete and tangible way, surviving made him anxious, as if his body had died. He only lived on the inside and lost the enthusiasm to come in touch with other lives. The feeling that he got lucky made him turn to enthusiasm itself, which was compatible with its internality and was in turn controlled by it. As time passed by (painfully slowly), when he faced a number of equally concrete, tangible lives, he started to feel anxious about death, which he was once so close to, as if death in its unknown state shared the nihility of life. Luo Ke, astonished at this, assumed that his dream, love and unnamable pursuit were similarly interactive, all of which made him feel like a widower. Immersed in it, he felt more deeply about everything away from him, as if in a mild trance. He was always thinking, thinking of another woman, another time, and another place, and therefore he was always absent-minded and unable to focus and ended up losing everything he had and falling into a new trance.

14

The second morning after Luo Ke and Ou Xiaolin went to the city D, an airmail letter from Sidney was put in the Yins' mailbox. The exquisite envelope stayed in the small and dark mailbox until the next morning for Yin Chu did not go downstairs for a whole day due to both physical and mental discomfort. She finally read the letter filled with Sun Shu's crooked Chinese characters, at almost the same time when Luo Ke was writing to her.

The woman Luo Ke had been pining for was buried in the several pieces of paper.

It was a clear morning, with brilliant sunlight. Yin Mang

got on the train at Creek station alone, where she was sixty kilometers away from Sydney. No one knew why she went there. She didn't even leave a note before leaving at noon the day before. The smell of the southeast trade wind from the Tasman Sea was vaguely present in the air of the temperate oceanic climate zone, and the famous opera house glittered in the harbor. Yin Mang got off and hurried to take the underground. Nobody knew when, perhaps near noon. Neither did anyone know where she wanted to go. After the accident happened, a witness said she was standing on the platform edge, constantly crossing and uncrossing her legs, and then a middle-aged man with a copy of the *Daily Telegraph* under his arm walked over and pushed her down the moment before the train came. In the chaos the man left as if nothing had happened and soon disappeared in the panicked crowd. Nobody remembered what he looked like. Only an old lady vaguely recalled that the newspaper he had was published in 1972, because he had been standing next to her before he walked towards Yin Mang. She thought he probably had coprolalia, for he never stopped cursing.

There were no more details and there never would be.

A photo was enclosed, in which there was a wind chime hanging by the window, and on the back of the photo was a line in Luo Ke's handwriting, "I love Luo Ke." It was the only thing related to him in the things Yin Mang left behind. Sun Shu asked Yin Mang's family to give it to Luo Ke.

Yin Chu dropped the letter and the photo on the sofa. She felt extremely, truly disappointed, which overwhelmed all the other emotions. The tragic scene was beyond her imagination and she was unable to stand that she could not see it with her own eyes. She walked to the kitchen, poured a glass of water and curled up in the sofa, weeping, as if there were another language in the weeping that described Yin Mang's disaster.

"I can't see." She was telling herself that she was not there and it was not possible, either.

"I can't see." She meant she parted with her sister, forever.

It was a long while before she suddenly thought of something. She took out the wrinkled photo under her bottom, smoothed it and started to examine it. But it did not contain any information about Australia because it was taken in Luo Ke's room. "It was meant to be this image," she thought.

15

"I want to take you to my childhood haunt, though it's a lot different now. There are many new buildings, places for tourists to change clothes, and new roads, and the beach is cleaned up too. Do you want to go?"

"No, only film crews go there."

Later they repeated the conversation, except that Luo Ke added, "Just go. I'll be fine staying in the room and thinking about the beach."

He pictured the beach, the sea in both turbulent and peaceful states, the waves rolling onto the shore incessantly as if they were kissing, and the beach turning desolate when the tourists left. He thought of the wide streets in this coastal city and of how he stayed dispirited in a room by the sea with this woman standing in front of the window, satisfied with their stagnation. Last night or dawn, when they snuggled up in bed, he felt like walking across the city. But now, he preferred to look from a distance. He was averse to visiting any place related with her childhood, because the past was always overflowing with meaning, or rather, meaninglessness. He would rather stay in a movie theater alone and watch her feature movie, watching her utter lines in costume and move in fake scenes. He waited in suspense until she appeared at the fifth minute. Before her logical death at the one hundred and fifteenth minute, she cried twice and came on the brink of crying once. At the sixteenth minute she kissed a man in an overcoat and rode a shiny bicycle through an alley at the forty-ninth minute. Only one minute later she appeared on the beach in a swimming suit, facing the sea and playing with the water, with her back to the audience. Luo Ke was familiar with the scene. The flirty woman on the screen was less elusive than the sulky one standing by the window at the moment. She was plain and simple on the screen, though she kept blabbering inexplicable words. The lines that demonstrated tenacity beyond the audience made her artificialities look adorable.

He came to her side and whispered "beach." He asked whether it was time for the tide to recede. "I don't know," she said. "Why did I come here?" "Ask yourself." "Perhaps I did come here for the beach, but I've never been there. Why?" "No one knows."

She turned around and touched his eyes, her fingers moving extremely slowly as if it were an intricate, unfamiliar move. He felt that her fingertips were so perfect, well-proportioned, and depressing.

She said meaningless things in a low voice by his side, uttering the syllables incessantly. They stood for a long time in the sunlight that passed through the window, savoring the joy that was about to come. Her fingers were still exploring and looking for something, as if indulging in the texture of silk and water. She thought she was happy to be there, to accept a gift, to accept the same gift many times, and to engrave it on her mind as if it were a festival.

"Beach," she said this word inadvertently, as if it were a hint or something philosophical, indicating that there were more to follow. At that moment she could not find anything that she could depend on, and therefore she said the word again, "Beach," which sounded hypnotic with the acquiescent sense of indulgence. Listen to the word, "beach." Does it have a metallic sound, the full spectrum of sunlight, and the attributes of a dream? Or is it a platform of lust that washes away time scales? Its content is as boundless as sands, and its image contains the profound tranquility after all the motion and storms.

This word was what Luo Ke had been looking for. He knew

that it would appear sooner or later in its original form, simple yet rich. It remained aloof from the world, independent, delicate and charming. It walked towards him and suddenly revealed itself without hesitation. No one could remain untouched by it, as it was unreasonable and extremely simple.

"You are the one that I have been craving for. He walks so casually as if he might lie on the ground in any minute. There is a vague sense of unluckiness in his look, which shocks me. Few people could remain infatuated with this quality for a long time. It neither belongs to his appearance nor to his nature. It's hard to describe, like something bleached and dyed."

"It's difficult for you to imagine how I feel for you. I just flipped. You were wearing a sport suit, standing on the wooden floor with Yin Chu. You looked fit, natural and full of vitality. Then came your obscenities, which were quite unexpected. And that exaggerated tone seemed to give you moral defense. I started to have feelings, right from here."

"Here."

"Yes, where else could it be?"

They cuddled each other, unaware of the passage of time. The light in the sky held out for a long time, and gradually, the clouds appeared and turned down the light. There was an indistinct scent of soap in the twilight, and then everything merged into the darkness.

Her fingers kept sliding over his skin and traced the contours of his whole body, feeling apologetic to some parts of his body and attached to some others. Her desire slowly infiltrated into his body and was then welcomed, retained and integrated into it. It constantly changed in shape, like a view blocked by a hedge. Trees on the dunes gently swung in the wind, and horses galloped on the vast plain beyond, like the heart pounding. Refined and graceful, they were having a conversation in a courteous manner interspersed with laughter. They carried out the straightforward process of deduction with sincerity and patience, and from time to time looked at the rippling water or the trace of the wind. Eventually they found nothing and stopped kissing with weariness and empty hands.

"But the beach …" she said.

"That's your childhood haunt."

16

Luo Ke didn't go to the beach before leaving the city D. Neither of them mentioned it again. Not that they were being evasive, but that they just forgot. Ou Xiaolin was always heading to the post office to make trunk calls because she was going to shoot a new movie in Shenzhen, Guangdong Province. Luo Ke finally took a tramcar ride and jumped off halfway. He browsed through a bookstore with a dusty façade without buying anything, and went out with his hand cut by a nail on the doorframe.

"Time to go home," he said to himself.

Luo Ke did not say goodbye to Ou Xiaolin's mother. He said it was uncommon, which she didn't understand. She saw him off at the port. When they shook hands, Luo Ke suddenly said, "A long time ago, Tao Lie sailed southwards along this coastline."

"Tao Lie? Who is he?"

"I've been wondering that too."

"Are you joking?"

"Yes, I might be." He smiled and thought it was like a dream.

He saw some small waves breaking around the ship, people saying goodbye on the port without unusual hubbubs, and the passenger ship anchored there motionless as if it did not intend to set sail. A seaman was walking back and forth on the afterdeck with a relaxed look on his face. There was nothing special to be found about this sail among innumerous others. "Then perhaps it could be called an immortal sail," Luo Ke thought.

"Write to me when you finish shooting the movie."

"I don't know how to write. I'm a lousy letter writer. You know what I mean? I'm terrible at it. It annoys me."

"Then call me. Well, no, just let me find you in some movie."

"You probably won't recognize me," she alerted him.

"No, you have your traits."

"Like what?" She seemed interested.

"I don't know. I just think I'll recognize you."

Luo Ke patted her on the head and walked towards the entrance.

"You ruined my hair," she said. He didn't hear nor did he turn around.

17

The ship moved slowly, as if it was sailing against the wind. Most of the time it was overcast. The sunlight was blocked by clouds and yet still sensible. Luo Ke was eating in the noisy canteen, absent-minded. The ship sailed between 120 and 125 degrees east longitude and the whole voyage covered about 522 nautical miles, southward. But he was unable to tell that, as the view never changed. He had been agonizing over such unspeakable feelings as the last confession of a dying believer. It was like a name, a city's name. Faced with the apathetic vast sea, he suddenly felt the impulse to speak. He felt that it was like uttering a person's name which had to be repeated and at the same time listened to reverently. He would find its true meaning someday.

Sailing southwards, he was unaware of the time, whether it was dawn, noon or evening. His loneliness was only occasionally interrupted by the dusty daylight and the nights accompanied by the sound of waves. In the semi-enclosed space moving slowly, people roamed around every accessible corner. Their loneliness was more overwhelming than the tiring boredom of the journey.

After dinner, boisterous dance music was played in the canteen. Some people at the door or outside the window were peeping inside. The place where they had dinner became a dance floor, on which a couple was enjoying their waltz in a mixed smell of cabbage and hot and sour soup. Luo Ke thought he and everything around him were mutually sarcastic without any profundity. They would forget each other as if they had never existed.

Luo Ke failed to have a sound sleep this night. A funeral gloom hung over the ancient sea that concealed tempestuous waves, which reminded him that something was awaiting him. He would walk up with a leisurely gait to welcome it again, to welcome a mistake as if it were victory. He would still be too occupied to appreciate its craziness and sweetness. It was a bourgeois luxury he did not think he could ever have. He would only continue the lament of Karl Shapiro in his record of exile, "Let the wind blow, for many a man shall die." He first received such everlasting comfort in his father's letter at the staging area full of mosquitoes and miasma in Vietnam. How old was he, sixteen or seventeen? Standing on the ground which had just been bombarded, he missed his mother land and missed the stairs with six turnings, the rainy seasons in which he stood in front of the window, the old red brick houses, the faded walls painted with flowery patterns, and the fences coated with tung oil. He wanted to go back there, to start a family and to die there in the end.

Time elapsed and a false sense of comfort corroded him. The craving for pleasure was rooted in his heart, as he was now surrounded by the sea. It was as if everything had happened, with only a few still hidden. He and the big world were able to forgive each other, because he saw no significance whatsoever in his way of living.

He thought of Xiang An, without the need of a similar figure to facilitate his imagination. She appeared and disappeared so quickly that he hardly had time to react. When she smiled, her features turned into a giant empty hole that extended inward through her heart to her private parts. Her charm eclipsed other cravings and her nudity dominated countless moments of commitments, which rendered him unable to gain insight into her heart. Their love was so illusory in that doomed summer.

They depended on each other as if one were the other's boat in a river, receiving all the instructions, hints, pressures, appeals and the tender affection. Everyone was a somber backflow instead of a gentle shore, splashing against the wall of affection and giving off loving signals just to demonstrate that they were so latently desperate and persistent.

Such relationships always gave him a sense of shame, like violent looting, while he couldn't afford thorough consideration in this aspect, as after all it involved the tear-jerking amorous desire.

From one summer to the next, a complete annual ring had grown in the trunk of an invisible tree of life. They were implanted into each other with a lasting sense of attachment, unaffected by the heat wave. They craved for each other's body and talked about private matters over the phone, with the common three-word nonsense which they could not help saying. "Are you crazy?" They heard each other.

After the four seasons, their bodies had been covered with love bites, sleep deprivation creeping into their kidneys, lungs and heart, and all forms of imploration had come down to illusion. The degree of closeness dropped to the bottom, and time resumed its position and again demonstrated its harshness and infinity. Like a traveler, he must be prepared for delays, though staying on the sea still made him anxious. The ending seemed to be in a loop. It was horrible to live like a dead man, to suffocate, and to ascend to heaven.

End. Darkness and light ended at the same time. He said to her that he was like her father and she was like his daughter, who would finally leave him after being created, nurtured, cultivated, groomed, appreciated and then missed by him.

With her stubborn childishness, she could be anyone's daughter. She once addressed him in the most intimate manner by calling him "dad" while crying.

Luo Ke lost her when she eloped.

"Go, my daughter." He tried to learn to send good wishes.

"Don't fall asleep," he said to himself, "or you'll dream of Siren singing."

18

Luo Ke got off near the square at downtown. He was back in this city with a dense population. The library bell tower stood with its flank facing the square. It would be there forever, he said to himself, at least for more than an age to witness all the joy and sorrow.

People were all walking in a hurry. The influence of winter began to manifest itself—the chill, the bored look on people's face, the sign to take health tonics, the red hue on the nose, the frequently-used handkerchiefs, and the phlegm on the pavement. Several blond Europeans were striding on the slow lane like purchasers from other provinces. Some travelers walked listlessly with drooping eyelids as if they had come to the wrong place, though they still held firmly the tour map in their hands with bulging veins like a treasure hunter in a backwater.

Luo Ke was familiar with these scenes, which formed a backdrop to his confusion. He called Yin Chu, and the phone rang in her room for a long time as if helping him to inquire. No one picked up. It was almost five in the afternoon. Where would she go? Luo Ke jumped on a tramcar again. The carriage was painfully packed with all sorts of people, some of whom cursed from time to time to release their anxiety. More people remained silent most of time, no matter how hard they were pushed and rubbed. They didn't utter a word, as if waiting for a dream guide to appear in what little space left in the carriage. They stood there with equanimity and without the slightest trace of surprise on their face. All of a sudden, they rushed off in swarms and disappeared in a twinkling of an eye.

The Xicun Apartment was now draped in darkness, with a strange pale purple shimmer from its brown gravel wall. There were few people on the street, which resembled a suburban scene. Suffering from travel fatigue, Luo Ke groped his way up the stairs in the darkness and suddenly felt as if he had strayed into this earthly world. He was uncertain about what he was doing and wondered what it meant. He pondered alone in the darkness, like a watchman strolling on the deserted street, surrounded by snores and midnight dreams. People relaxed their body and mind in light or deep sleep, their inaudible words wafting to Luo Ke as hypnotic greetings, which deprived him of the sense of time and everything related with his inner world. He vaguely recalled the floral shops which were about to close, the sprinkler on the shelf, the colored paper slips in the tin bucket, and the dark red rose buds behind the window. He should have bought one even though he had no change in his pocket. Luo Ke only thought of this romantic plan when he was about to knock on the door.

Everything was normal, before anything astonishing happened. Yin Chu opened the door, and they came inside after exchanging lukewarm greetings. Yin Chu was cooking in the kitchen, with the smell of rice mixed with eggs and sausages drifting in the air. Luo Ke did not mention the imaginary rose. Like a husband in a happy marriage, he paid due attention to the meaning of the things that did not happen in his life, knowing when to contain his own indulgence and, most importantly, his imagination.

In the south, the cold, damp winter was a ubiquitous menace, filling all the houses with freezing air. Everything within reach was cold and hard. People walked in the room while their heart remained undisturbed as still water. The faint, warm flickering flame of yearning in the room surrounded Luo Ke and Yin Chu with a dim sense of narrative after trudging through the emotional swamp. It demonstrated the desolation of the universe, the triviality of life and their misplaced autumnal confusion and, at the same time, complemented their loneliness and the aesthetic of their interdependence. They stared at each other, indulging in each other's company. They seemed to be aware of their elusive, hopeless relationship which hovered between speculation and understanding. It was different, as it was more lasting than hatred, stronger than desire, more covert than attachment, and more desolate than pain. It was there to stay once it emerged between them. It was an impulse from time immemorial, as solid as a rock, though without an ending. Sometimes it was as gentle and refreshing as raindrops that fell on one's face.

"There was a letter from Sun Shu," Yin Chu said.

"About Yin Mang?"

"Do you want to read it now?"

"What does it say?" Luo Ke considered for a moment and realized such messages had always been relayed to him. "I'd rather not read it myself. Can you tell me?"

Yin Chu slowly retold what was in the letter, and the illusory first-person perspective confused her, as if she had experienced Yin Mang's life and the moment she died, her voice full of genuine grief.

"I love her as much as you do," she said in the end.

"You can't prove it." Luo Ke said, after a long time of silence, "Who can tell us the stories of our love and death? We don't even have the time to listen to our own heart. We live and die where we don't live. We have no choice but to see our hard-earned relationship go away. Because there are no special marks, we soon begin to neglect each other, and when we regret and falter, we feel as if we only live for some mark, which is rooted in our heart, someplace beyond our reach where we don't exist. The one and only gathering in our life, which involves all of our affections, appears to be real for its illusory extension. It's the consummate moment in our life, like a prayer full of expectations for the destination and visceral longing for the afterlife." Luo Ke wanted to tell Yin Chu everything on his mind. Though it was as ideal and noble as the paradise in panpipe music, it was also beyond verbal description and gradually died out when he pondered it.

Luo Ke averted his eyes from Yin Chu's face.

"You don't want to know how Ou Xiaolin is?"

"No," she said, "why don't you ask how I am?"

"OK. How are you?" Luo Ke didn't look at her, as he was sure that she must be looking at him in an unbearable way.

"I was waiting for you to come back."

"Nobody does this," he said, eyes still averting.

"I know I didn't have to. But I know you have nowhere else to go."

"Why?"

"I don't know. Perhaps because you look like a wanderer."

"That's not convincing."

"Yes, it is. Everyone who has ever made love with you can see that. Nobody is afraid of losing you." She believed it was true. Luo Ke was a pigeon flying in the house whose purity was confined in this place. He was also a camel in the bedroom with the distance of its lonely trudge limited. There was a broad backdrop to his affection, but it was a pre-set distraction, like a view through a window or a still life in a frame. He owned it, indulged in its beauty but would never reach out to touch it. His love concerned himself. His attachment misled him into thinking that everyone and every situation was independent and that whether sex or any experience close to it was as absolute and indescribable as orgasm and death.

"Fine, verdict accepted." He still had no idea what it meant. He walked around in several rooms, then resumed his chair and continued the conversation. He figured even if nothing had happened, he would still be in the same state as now. He had never been shaped by life. "Is that true?" he asked Yin Chu.

"Someone said you lack boundaries."

"Who?"

"Yin Mang. You still won't read that letter?"

"So I convince myself of what happened, and then what? It defies logic. I think of it and it becomes noticeable, also disheartening. But I don't need it. It's so far away. Everything I think of, even myself, is so far away. Why does it matter whether it is true or not? I think of it, of everything, and revise them until they become a different version."

"You shock me," Yin Chu said worriedly.

"No, no," Luo Ke said, with an incomprehensible gesture, "that's not what I mean."

"It doesn't matter." Yin Chu stroked the skin of his hands, arms and his face, looking for the silence she was accustomed to.

"If we die, people apart from ourselves will have a structural satisfaction. If other people die, we feel that everything continues and nothing is interrupted. Pining is only an intention, which will be replaced by the intention to read, but it does not end. As good readers, we read intensively. But only when we fondle our beloved ones do we come closer to our heart and tilt toward ourselves ..."

"But I welcome you, if no one enters our heart like entering our bedroom ..."

"But we always narrate to each other ..."

"If we just come ..."

"If we only have beginnings and happy endings, there will also be regret ..."

"You know what I mean," he said to her.

Stories by Contemporary Writers from Shanghai

A Nest of Nine Boxes
Jin Yucheng

A Pair of Jade Frogs
Ye Xin

Ah, Blue Bird
Lu Xing'er

Beautiful Days
Teng Xiaolan

Between Confidantes
Chen Danyan

Breathing
Sun Ganlu

Calling Back the Spirit of the Dead
Peng Ruigao

Dissipation
Tang Ying

Folk Song
Li Xiao

Forty Roses
Sun Yong

Game Point
Xiao Bai

Gone with the River Mist
Yao Emei

Goodby, Xu Hu!
Zhao Changtian

His One and Only
Wang Xiaoyu

Labyrinth of the Past
Zhang Yiwei

Memory and Oblivion
Wang Zhousheng

No Sail on the Western Sea
Ma Yuan

Normal People
Shen Shanzeng

Paradise on Earth
Zhu Lin

Platinum Passport
Zhu Xiaolin

River under the Eaves
Yin Huifen

She She
Zou Zou

The Confession of a Bear
Sun Wei

The Eaglewood Pavilion
Ruan Haibiao

The Elephant
Chen Cun

The Little Restaurant
Wang Anyi

The Messenger's Letter
Sun Ganlu

The Most Beautiful Face in the World
Xue Shu

There Is No If
Su De

Vicissitudes of Life
Wang Xiaoying

When a Baby Is Born
Cheng Naishan

White Michelia
Pan Xiangli